How to
Get Rid of
Your
Older Brother

How to Get Rid of Your Older Brother

Joel L. Schwartz

A YEARLING BOOK

Published by
Dell Publishing
a division of
Bantam Doubleday Dell Publishing Group, Inc.
666 Fifth Avenue
New York, New York 10103

The trademark Yearling® is registered in the U.S. Patent and Trademark Office.
The trademark Dell® is registered in the U.S. Patent and Trademark Office.

ISBN: 0-440-40623-4

Printed in the United States of America

May 1992

10 9 8 7 6 5 4 3 2 1

OPM

To my little brother Alan.
Some people put their foot in their mouth. You put your foot through the ceiling.

Special thanks to Uncle Marshall for his help on the sports scenes and for buying the telephone brick.
And to the brothers who told it like it was:

BIG	LITTLE
Jeff	Steve
Doug	Jon
Scott	Todd
Stan	Bruce
Mike	Richie

◀ 1 ▶

My name is Jay, but everyone calls me Kipper. You may think it's short for Skipper, but it's not. When my older brother, Louis, was three and I was one and a half, he told my parents he wanted to trade me in for a dog. Why anyone would want to get rid of the best younger brother an older brother could have is beyond me, but that's what Louis wanted to do. Since getting rid of me was not possible, he did the next best thing. He started ordering me around and calling me *Kipper*, after the Irish setter that lived around the corner from us. By the time I found out I was named for a dog, everyone was so used to calling me Kipper there was no way I could change it.

I guess things could have been worse. The dog could have been a Lhasa apso named Muffy. You'd think that

Louis would have let up on me a little when he finally got a dog, but he didn't. Instead he ordered both of us around. Waldo didn't seem to mind it as much as I did. Louis would be yelling things at him and he'd just sit there, wide-eyed, head cocked to the side, and yawn. The louder Louis would yell the wider Waldo's eyes would get but in the end he wouldn't budge. Soon I was cocking my head to the side and staring wide-eyed into Louis's face and doing nothing. Boy, did Louis get mad at us both.

Even so, it hasn't been easy being Louis's younger brother for the past twelve years. Last night was a typical example. We had just sat down to eat dinner when Louis started.

"Mom, you'll never guess what happened when I went to the supermarket for you today," said Louis.

"What happened?" asked Mom.

"Hmm?" mumbled Pop, who seemed more interested in watching the nightly news.

Louis looked over at me to make sure I was listening before he continued. He had a big fat smirk on his face. "I was waiting in line at the deli counter to get some baloney when this fat lady pointed to a piece of kippered salmon in the case and asked to see it up close. When the guy behind the counter showed it to her she said it wasn't fresh because it didn't look flaky enough. I told her that we had a very flaky Kipper at our house that she could have for free."

Louis thinks that's funny but that just goes along with his dumb way of looking at things. He has other strange ways of looking at things. In his mind he also believes he has free access to anything of mine, while anything of his is off limits. For obvious reasons I never argue with this deranged logic. Instead I cock my head to the side, stare wide-eyed into Louis's face, and silently make plans to get what I want from his room before he gets up the next day.

It was 6:00 A.M. and I was crawling silently on my hands and knees into enemy territory. My objective: a gray and maroon football jersey in the bottom drawer of the brown dresser on the opposite side of Louis's room. Down the hall I could hear the machine-gun sound of my father's snoring resonating from my parents' room.

The path to the dresser was an obstacle course of muddy sneakers and dirty underwear. Under the last pair of dirty underpants, quite by accident, I found five crumpled pictures from the *Sports Illustrated* swimsuit issue. I smiled at this unexpected bonus and stuffed them quietly in my shirt.

Without warning a wild savage beast sprang at me from nowhere and began to lick my left ear unmercifully. I patted Waldo on the head and prayed that he wouldn't get too excited and bark. Finally Waldo finished licking every ounce of dog yummy from my ear and returned to the warmth and darkness of the cave under my brother's bed.

I got up on my elbows and peered at my brother's clock radio. 6:10. I'd have to work quickly. I checked my brother once more just to make sure he was still sound asleep, then gave his bottom dresser drawer a yank. Rats, stuck. I tugged a little harder but it still refused to move. In desperation I quietly got up on my knees, took a deep breath, and pulled with all my might. This time the drawer offered no resistance, and before I could stop myself, I was tumbling backward and all my brother's sweatshirts were airborne.

6:15. *The weather forecast for today is cloudy and raining sweatshirts.* One landed on Waldo's head as he peeked out to see what was going on. Three landed on my brother's desk across the room, and the gray and maroon football jersey landed on my brother's face just as he was sitting up in bed.

This gave me a little head start, but two steps away from the safety of my room Louis caught up with me and pinned me to the floor. Holding a clenched fist inches away from my nose he yelled, "If I ever catch you in my room again I'm going to kill you!"

I guess Louis is not a morning person. But that's typical of Louis. He thinks that because he's a year and a half older, six inches taller, and much stronger, he owns the house.

"Do I make myself clear?" he snapped through half gritted teeth. *My, what pretty teeth you have! Did you brush today using a tartar control formula?* I knew if I said that I'd lose my life instantly. Instead I forced a smile, tried not to look too afraid, and prayed that one parent would magically appear to rescue me.

Then Louis let go of my arms. With a combination of daring and stupidity I swatted his fist away and shrieked, "If you kill me they'll put you in jail for life and I won't come to visit you ever." With the full force of my twenty extra pounds I tried unsuccessfully to throw him off.

Louis smiled. "You couldn't come to visit me anyway because you'd be dead."

"Even if I were dead," I repeated confidently as if what I was going to say next made perfectly good sense, "I still wouldn't come, and if I ever catch *you* in *my* room you're dead meat."

"Oh yeah?" said Louis, making a fist again. "And who do you think is going to enforce that! Huh?" The eyeball-to-eyeball who-will-blink-first contest was now officially on. *What was taking my parents so long?* .

Louis pulled his hand back again and looked about to bop me one when a door opened down the hall and out staggered my father.

"Kipper was taking things from my room again," said Louis.

His word against mine. "I was not. I was on my way to the bathroom and Louis tackled me for no reason." He did tackle me.

Using the wall as a guide, my father made his way down the hall. I could tell he was still half asleep since we were tangled up on the floor and he was shouting at the wall. "I don't care who did what to whom. Go in your rooms and get dressed. Thank God school starts again today. The two of you have been at each other's throats all summer."

"But, Dad," Louis protested as he dug his knee into my thigh one more time for good luck before he climbed off, "Kipper always . . ."

"Louis just dug his . . ."

My father continued to yell at the wall. "I don't want to hear it. Get dressed!"

"You wait," said Louis as he disappeared into his room and slammed the door.

I waited quietly in the hall for a minute before walking down to Louis's room and knocking. "Can I borrow your gray and maroon football jersey?" Without waiting for an answer I ran back to my room, managing to get the door shut a micro-millisecond before something came crashing against it. I heard my parents' door open and my father ask, "Louis, what's your muddy sneaker doing in the hall next to Kipper's door?" I turned my radio on just then so I never got to hear Louis's reply. It was a good question though.

◀ 2 ▶

For the life of me I don't know why Louis complains so much. He's the one that gets to do things first. He's definitely my parents' favorite, with the dog a close second. He's got a great little brother. What else does he want?

"Kipper, breakfast is ready."

"I'll be right down, Mom," I replied. "Greeble frednatz blingee minkee."

"What did you say?" she yelled back. I was laughing too hard to answer. "What did you say?" Mom is so much fun to fool with in the morning.

Downstairs Louis was already sitting at the kitchen table and just for spite he was wearing the gray and maroon football jersey.

"What did you say?" she asked again.

"I said, 'Greeble frednatz blingee minkee.' "

"I thought so," she said. "Hurry up and eat your breakfast or you'll be late."

I sat down opposite Louis and pointed to the cereal. "Mmmmuh!"

Louis handed it to me and pointed to the juice. "Mmmmuh!"

I pushed the plastic pitcher toward him and pointed to the sugar and cream. "Mmmmuh! Mmmmuh!"

The cream and sugar came sliding over. "Mmm-muh! Mmmmuh!"

I passed Louis the bread and butter.

"Louis and Kipper! Cut that out right now or I'll be forced to do something that neither of you will like."

It's hard to take my mother seriously in the morning. I mean, how worried would you be when those threatening words came from someone who was wearing bunny rabbit slippers? I looked down at my cereal knowing that if I looked over at Louis I'd burst out laughing.

Today was a very important day in my life because it was the first day of junior high school. No more fooling around. This was when things started to count for real. There are a lot of things to consider when you go to a new school. For example, how difficult will it be to find your way around the school? Louis had promised to show me where my first-period class was but I guessed I could forget about that now. Even if he did tell me where it was, knowing him I'd probably end up in the basement or the boys' room. Then you have to wonder if you'll have enough time to get from class to class. What if one class is in the basement and your next class is on the second floor on the opposite side of the school behind two other classrooms and up an extra set of steps? Is it possible to get there in four minutes? What if I can't get the combination on my locker to work? What if I get it to work but my locker won't open anyway? What if I get the lock to work and the locker opens but I forgot my notebook at home? And then there are the important worries. Will I find a girl short enough to go out with? What if she's taller but likes me anyway? What if she's the right size but she's already in eighth grade? Maybe I'd be sick today.

"We're late!" said Louis, as he sprang up from the table. I grabbed a jelly donut and followed Louis out the door. Louis was in a half walk, half trot and it was tough keeping up with him. After a while I didn't even try.

I arrived at the bus stop just as the bus pulled up. I got on behind Louis, who headed for the back of the bus.

"Where do you think you're going?" he asked. I opened my mouth to answer as he pointed to the back of the bus and said, "This is only for ninth graders. Seventh graders sit up there in front." The guys on the backseat roared their approval. I wanted to charge past him and grab one seat but it was four of them against one of me, so I reluctantly found a seat in the second row next to a skinny boy with pimples.

Go ahead, show off for your friends. Your day will come. It was a short ride to the school. As soon as the bus pulled up to the platform, I checked my roster card once again and headed for the closest door. Room 200 was easier to find than I expected. I sat down in the back and looked around the room. Since three elementary school sixth grade classes joined together to form this seventh grade class I only knew a few of the kids. To me it looked like the usual mix: three dweebs with glasses, three dweebettes—two with glasses, one without—two short fat boys, two tall boys, one fat girl, two very tall girls, four cool guys including me, and five cool-looking girls. I often wonder what the dweebs think when they look over the class. Hmmmm: three cool kids with glasses, three cool girls—two with glasses, one without—two short fat dweebs, two tall skinny dorks, three gross-looking girls, four stuck-up guys, and five girls who think they're too good for everybody.

At the front of the room sitting cross-legged on the top of his desk was my homeroom teacher. He had a small black book in his hand. "Welcome. My name is Mr. Gross. I'll be your homeroom teacher this year, and for some of you, your math teacher too. When I call your name raise your hand so I can get to know you. Arnold Bernstein." I think the first day of school is always a big waste of time. The teachers call the roll, give out the books, and then say "Talk quietly among yourselves" while they sit back in their chairs and think about their summer vacation. The second most wasted day is the last. The teachers collect the books, give back the projects you gave them at Christmastime, and then say "Talk quietly among yourselves" while they sit back in their chairs and think about their summer vacation.

"Marshall Friedenberg."

If it were up to me I'd eliminate them both. But then there'd be another first and last day, which I'd have to get rid of also. And another, and another until there'd be . . . no school. No school . . . hooray!

"Jay Scott?"

I would have probably continued daydreaming if one of the kids from my elementary school hadn't poked me in the arm and pointed to the front of the room.

"Jay Scott."

"Huh . . . ? Oh, here . . . here."

"Stand up, Jay, so I can see who you are."

I stood up and half covered my face with my hand. Everyone around me was giggling. Great way to start the year, Jay, I thought. As I started to sit down the teacher asked, "Do you have an older brother named Louis?" I nodded. "He was in my math class when he was in seventh grade." I nodded again. "What a great student he was." I knew what was coming next. "You're going to have to work pretty hard to do as well as he did."

I forced a smile and sat down. Everyone thinks Louis is terrific. After all, he's smart in school, he was elected president of his eighth grade class last year, he's the number one running back on the football team, and every girl that sees him wants to go out with him. Maybe Mr. Gross should live with us for a while and see if he still thinks Louis is so great. The best time to come would be during the cold weather. Louis's nose starts to run October first and doesn't stop until April fifteenth. The noises Louis makes with his nose, usually during mealtime, are a treat for the ears and a torment to the appetite. Or maybe Mr. Gross should try to borrow Louis's gray and maroon jersey. He'd change his mind about Louis pretty quick.

I didn't hear much of what Mr. Gross had to say after that. I was too busy looking out the window and daydreaming. In my dream I was the star running back and Louis was the manager of the team. There were two minutes to go in the game, we were behind by five points, and the coach had just called a time-out. In the huddle the coach diagramed a running play that could win the game for us. Louis stood outside the huddle, bucket in one hand, towels in the other, waiting to give out drinks. "Good luck, Jay. I know you can win the game for us," said Louis. The team lined up and the quarterback handed me the ball. I ran to the left behind two blockers, cut back to the right, twisted, spun, dodged, and powered my way forward. I could see the goal line in front of me when . . . Riiiiinnnnng. Homeroom was over. I looked at the roster card. Oh *no*. My next class was on the second floor on the opposite side . . .

◀ **3** ▶

When Louis and I were younger my parents would have Wanda Plimpkin, one of the neighborhood girls, come over and baby-sit for us but that stopped two years ago. It wasn't just because my parents thought Louis was old enough to be on his own, they were sort of forced into it.

Wanda, who was then a senior in high school, had been our steady baby-sitter since she was in eighth grade. She was short and fat and her face was frozen in a perpetual frown. On her back, like a misshapen hump, she always carried a pukey green book bag, crammed to the gills with books and school accessories. We called her Blimpkin the munchkin. Over the years, if she said one thousand words total to Louis and me, that was a lot, and most of the thousand were probably *"Keep it down!"* There are very few things Louis and I agree on but our feelings about Wanda were unanimous. We hated her.

One particular night Wanda had sent us up to our rooms early because we were making too much noise. We vowed revenge. Just after eleven Wanda fell asleep on the sofa. As I snuck down quietly and tied her shoelaces together, Louis went into my parents' room and dialed our other phone line. I scurried up the stairs, grabbed a camera from my closet, and joined Louis at the top of the stairs to watch. I had just focused my camera when Wanda awoke with a start (click) and leaped to her feet (click). As she took her first step her feet were jerked out from under her (click) and she fell sideways (click) onto the coffee table, splitting it in two (click). Wanda was so embarrassed (click) she grabbed her books (click) and ran out of the house in tears (click) (click) (click). Louis and I felt bad for about five minutes. Sometimes we can be pretty mean.

Louis has been sitting for me ever since and it hasn't been that bad until tonight. Things started out the way they did most Saturday nights. Mom was yelling at Dad because he wasn't going to be ready on time. Dad was yelling at Mom because he couldn't find a shirt to match his tie and jacket. I was yelling at Louis because he was taking something from my room, or was it the other way around?

My parents left in a huff at eight o'clock and all was quiet. "I'll be watching TV," I announced. I heard running footsteps behind me and Louis charged past me into the den. By the time I caught up with him, he was firmly planted on the sofa and waving the remote control.

"I get the remote first tonight," I cried.

"Really," he replied as he continued to flip channels.

"I have to watch something on channel twelve at eight-thirty for social studies," I said.

"Watch it on the TV in the basement," he replied.

"That TV is no good," I said.

"You said it was good enough for me to watch yesterday so why isn't it good enough for you today?" asked Louis.

"Then can I use the remote for a second to see one thing?" I asked calmly.

"If I give you the remote that'll be the last I'll see of it for tonight."

"No big deal," I replied as I walked into the kitchen and noisily opened the refrigerator. "Mmmmm, is this good. Mmmmmmmm! Look at that, mmmmmmmmm! Mom got that too, mmmmmmmmmm! Mmmmmmmmm. Is this good."

"What is?" asked Louis.

"Nothing," I said. "Mmmmmmm!" I opened the refrigerator twice more and clanked a spoon in a dish and on a glass.

"What're you eating?" asked Louis again.

"You wouldn't be interested," I said. "Just some double chocolate royal ice cream and hot fudge sauce."

"I didn't see anything like that when I looked into the refrigerator before," said Louis.

"That's because it was in the freezer," I replied.

"Forget it, it's no big deal." I was eating a large bowl of fudge-covered ice cream when Louis appeared, remote control still in his hand. Holding the remote tightly in his left hand, Louis grabbed the scooper in his right but quickly realized it would be impossible to scoop the ice cream one-handed because it was still too frozen. He put the remote down right in front of him so that I couldn't grab it, and he held the container still with one hand while he scooped with the other. After he filled his plate with two large scoops of ice cream he went over to a pot of fudge sauce simmering on the stove. Three spoonfuls pretty much covered everything, and he was deciding whether he should put on a fourth when he realized he had left the remote on the counter. I lunged for it.

"It's mine," yelled Louis as I got to the remote a step ahead of him. I folded my hands so he couldn't grab it back. "I had it first."

"You put it down so it's mine now," I said.

"I just went over to get some . . ." But I was already out of the kitchen, flipping channels in the den. Louis stomped after me into the den. "If you don't give me the remote back now I'll . . ." I ignored Louis completely, so he went back into the kitchen, got his uneaten plate of ice cream, and returned to the den. "This is your last chance to give it back," he yelled. Not only didn't I give it back, but I began to whistle "Who's Afraid of the Big Bad Wolf?"

His plate of ice cream plopped onto my head. Louis gave it an extra push down so it wouldn't fall off. The fudge sauce oozed down my neck.

"You look rather good with chocolate sideburns," said Louis. "Now give me the remote!"

I waved the remote in Louis's direction and calmly placed it in my shirt pocket. "No way!"

Louis's ears were bright red. "Give it to me!"

I took the empty ice cream plate off my head and flung it in his direction. Louis ducked and the plate sailed over his head, crashing into the den wall just below my father's high school graduation picture.

"Now you've had it," said Louis as he chased me around the sofa three times, and upstairs. I thought I had enough of a lead to get into my room and close the door but Louis managed to jam his foot in the door-way and stop me. It was his strength against my weight and for a while it was a standoff. Then Louis stopped and withdrew his foot as if he was giving up. I in turn took my hands away from the door and wiped my palms on my pants, and then the door flew open and smacked me squarely on the nose.

I don't know if I was knocked out or what but the next thing I remember was Louis kneeling down beside me holding a towel full of ice to my nose. The center of my face felt numb and all around where my nose should have been ached. I tried unsuccessfully to sit up.

"Are you all right?" asked Louis. He actually looked concerned. I tried to sit up again but my head was spinning badly so I lay back down. "Are you all right?"

"I'll live, I guess." This time I was able to sit up and look around. There was blood everywhere. "What happened?" I asked.

Louis looked very concerned. "The door must have hit your nose. You can breathe all right, can't you? It isn't broken, is it?"

Louis helped me up and I looked at myself in the mirror. My face was smeared with blood and my nose was bright red. *It's broken. Now I'm fat and deformed too.* I fingered it gently to make sure it wasn't crooked. Louis reached out to touch my nose but I wouldn't let him. "It was an accident," he said in a shaky voice. "I didn't mean it. Mom and Dad are going to kill me. What am I going to do?" I felt a little woozy so I sat down on my bed with my back up against the headboard for support.

Louis stared silently at the floor before disappearing downstairs. He returned in a minute carrying a bucket in one hand and a pile of rags in the other. He got down on his hands and knees and as he began scrubbing the blotched green rug repeated, "I'm dead. What are Mom and Dad going to do? It was an accident. I didn't mean it." Then for some strange reason, maybe out of fear, maybe out of compassion, maybe out of stupidity, I joined him scrubbing on the floor.

We worked together for over an hour, the silence only broken occasionally by my sniffing and Louis's heavy breathing. "I think it's all up," said Louis, standing up to get a better view. I stood up too. The rug looked wet but clean. I walked into the bathroom and cleaned up my face. Then I washed my T-shirt and hung it on the towel rack to dry.

Louis looked at his watch. "Are you sure you're all right?" I nodded. "Keep the ice on your nose and call me if you need anything. I'll be in the den watching TV. I hope I didn't miss the beginning of the movie.''

Glad I stopped bleeding before the movie started. Wouldn't want Louis to miss anything. I watched Louis disappear down the steps. *Enjoy the movie . . . you jerk.* I walked into my room and slammed the door and climbed into bed. *I'll get him.* Somewhere between that thought and planning what I would do I fell asleep.

‹4›

"I'll be taking the late bus home tonight," said Louis on his way out the door. "The first football team meeting is today."

I grabbed two pieces of toast and followed. "Me too," I echoed.

Louis turned around and pointed at me. "You're going out for football?" he asked with a big smile.

"Sure," I replied. "I'm going to open such big holes in the other team's line that even you will be able to run through them."

"Speaking of running, when did you learn how to run?" said Louis.

I took off in the direction of the bus stop. "I can beat you any day," I yelled over my shoulder. The surprise challenge gave me a slight lead at first and I pumped my arms and churned my legs furiously to keep my advantage.

Louis caught up to me easily within a block and he knocked my books out of my hand as he passed me. "Don't be late for the bus."

"You jerk." My side hurt and I had a tough time catching my breath. *Louis works out every day. That's why he can beat me now. In two weeks I'll be in shape and then we'll see who will win.*

I got to the bus stop just as the bus driver was ready to close the door. Louis was already sitting comfortably on the backseat. "The kippered turtle has arrived," he announced as I sat down. "What took you so long?"

I didn't even look at him. *Two weeks, Louis. You wait.*

During lunch I asked my best friend Don if he would go out for football with me.

"When did you get this sudden interest in football?" he asked.

"I've always been interested in playing," I replied.

"That's news to me. The only thing I ever thought you were interested in was taking pictures."

"I just never had the time," I said. "Come on and go out for it with me. It'll be fun."

"You have to be crazy to play football. The coach runs you into the ground during practices and the other teams run you into the ground during the games."

"You and I together," I replied. "It'll be fun."

"No thanks," said Don. "I'll have my fun watching you having fun, playing."

"All the girls love a football star."

"A shining star maybe," said Don, "but not a flattened one."

After school I walked down to the gym. Most of the kids that were sitting on the bleachers were eighth and ninth graders so I sat alone. Louis appeared a couple of minutes later, waved, and sat down with his teammates from last year.

To my surprise Mr. Gross, my homeroom teacher, came out of the coaching office and stood in front of us. "Welcome. Glad to see so many kids trying out for football this year. Those of you who are eighth or ninth graders must have a two-point-zero average or better to be eligible to play. Don't show up at the next practice and make me embarrass you, because I guarantee you, I will check. For those in seventh grade I'll be checking with your teachers too and if you're not working, I'll warn you first and if things don't get better, you're history."

Mr. Gross took a stack of green papers from his clipboard and passed them out. "In order to practice with the team you must return this form, completed, to me on Wednesday. One side of this form should be signed by your parents giving you permission to play and the other side signed by your family doctor saying that you are healthy enough to play. The school will provide all your equipment except socks, shoes, and an athletic supporter with a cup."

Coach Gross looked at me and then at Louis before he continued. "Practice begins every day promptly at three-fifteen and goes until five. Not everybody will play but all those who come out to practice regularly and work hard will make the team. Any questions?''

"How many games do we have and when are they?" asked a kid behind me.

"We have five games, all on Friday afternoons. The first one is three weeks from this Friday." Coach Gross looked around for any more questions and when there were none he said, "Okay, see everyone Wednesday," and he left.

I waited till Louis and his buddies left before I got up and went. Unfortunately we all took the same bus home.

"No way you'll ever pass the physical," yelled Louis as the guys around him roared with laughter.

"What size athletic cup do you use?" I replied. "Extra small or an aluminum-lined peanut shell?"

The battle lines were drawn. The one with the last cutting remark without a retort from the other was the winner.

"You'll need a special radar device to find yours!" said Louis.

"Funny, Louis. Funny. You ought to be on the stage. There's one leaving for Texas in the morning."

"What would you say if you could talk?"

"What do you hear from your brain?"

"You used that one last time," said Louis.

"You always say that when you can't think of anything else to say," I replied.

"You always say that when I catch you using something you used before," said Louis.

"You always say that when . . . forget it. Just don't get in my way when we scrimmage."

"I'm shaking," said Louis.

I didn't bother to reply. Actions speak louder than words.

"How's football going?" yelled Don as he saw me limping down the hall toward the lunchroom.

"Wonderful," I replied. "Every time I take a breath my back hurts, my legs hurt, my arms hurt, my ribs hurt, and my head hurts."

"When did practice start?" asked Don.

"Yesterday!"

"At this rate you'll be crippled by Friday," said Don.

I took Don's hand and ran it across a large bump on the back of my head. "Feel this. I'm growing another head. . . . Owww, not so hard."

"No pain, no gain," said Don.

"How much gain can this body take?" I asked.

"My dad always says people grow through painful experiences."

"At this rate I'll be seven feet two by the middle of next week," I replied.

"Wanna go to the movies Friday night?" asked Don.

I started to answer but shrill giggles down the hall caught my attention. Louis was surrounded by three girls who were all laughing at what he was saying. I pictured myself in Louis's place.

"Then I took the ice cream and dumped it on Louis's head. He looked rather cool in chocolate sideburns."

"You crack me up, Jay," said one girl.

"Your older brother acts like such a dweeb. How can you stand living with him?" asked another.

My eyes twinkled and my hair glistened in the sunlight. I stretched, aware that my muscles were straining the seams of my shirt. "It's not easy but I manage."

"Will you be the starting left tackle for the first game?" asked the third girl.

This time I just smiled and didn't answer.

"He is!" the girls shouted in unison. "See you at lunch, Jay. We'll save you a seat."

"Do you want to go or not?" asked Don again.

I looked over Don's shoulder again but Louis and the girls were gone. "Huh?"

"Earth to Jay. Earth to Jay," said Don sarcastically. "Do you want to go to the movies with me Friday night or not?"

"Yeah, sure. I think it's time I got a girlfriend," I said.

"What brought that up?" asked Don.

"I don't know," I replied. "It just sort of occurred to me. There's nothing wrong with that, is there?"

"No, I've thought about getting a girlfriend too but I never get around to it."

"I want her to be in eighth grade too," I said.

"Don't you know that eighth grade girls won't consider going out with a boy unless he's in at least ninth grade?"

"Who told you that?" I asked.

"My sister. She's in tenth grade so she ought to know."

"I can understand why an eighth grade girl wouldn't go out with an ordinary immature seventh grade boy but they haven't met me yet."

"Look out," yelled Don as he put his hand up to cover his face. "There's a stampede of eighth grade girls headed this way. We'll be trampled. Run for your life."

"You'll see," I replied confidently as we got into the lunch line. "Maybe I'll even try for a ninth grade girl."

As we got closer to the food Don pointed to some yellowish runny stuff on the hot dogs. "Yeech. What's that?"

"Cheese," I replied.

"What kind?" he asked.

"Machee cheese," I replied.

"Machee cheese?"

"It doubles as paste for papier-mâché projects in art."

"Next," said a lady in white with yellow cheese smeared on her apron.

I pointed to the hamburgers. "I'll take two of those and one baked potato."

When I reached the register the lady looked at my tray and told me I owed two dollars and seventy-five cents. As I got the money out of my pocket to pay she was already looking over Don's tray. In addition to the two hamburgers and baked potato he had gotten stewed tomatoes, a salad, a juice, and an oatmeal raisin cookie.

"Two dollars," said the lady.

"Two dollars?" I repeated in surprise. "He has twice as much as me on his tray. How come I have to pay seventy-five cents more?"

"You bought your food à la carte so it cost more. He got the whole lunch so it cost less," said the cashier.

"Oh, I get it," I replied. "If I go back and get some stewed tomatoes, a salad, juice, and an oatmeal raisin cookie, you'll give me seventy-five cents back."

"Too late," said the lady. "I already rang it up." I was still shaking my head in disbelief when Don got to the table.

"Want some stewed tomatoes?" he asked as he sat down.

I reached over and took his oatmeal cookie. "No thanks, but I'll take this."

"Hey, I wanted that," yelled Don.

"Too late," I said as I popped it into my mouth.

"You know," said Don, "I've been thinking . . ."

"Something new and original for you," I interjected.

"When you go to talk to the girl for the first time be calm and confident. Even though she's looking you over from head to toe don't let it bother you. She probably won't see your braces unless a rubber band breaks and hits her in the face. She'll never know your palms are sweaty unless you try to hold hands. She'll think you're very smart unless of course you open your mouth and try to talk to her. And if she gets sick initially because she doesn't like your looks hang in there because the waves of nausea usually pass in about fifteen or twenty minutes."

"I always get nervous when I have to face a girl for the first time and start the conversation."

"Let me get this straight," said Don. "You want the girl to begin the conversation and you don't want to be able to see her. That would be the world's greatest illusion if you could do it."

"Tell me about it unless . . . If I talked to a girl first on the phone then I wouldn't have to worry about having to look at her or having her gaping at me."

"That would work okay for the face-to-face part but the only way for her to begin the conversation is to get her to call you. How you going to do that?" asked Don.

"It was a good thought but wait . . . What do you think of this idea?"

◀ 6 ▶

"This is not going to work," said Don as he looked up and down the hall once more to make sure no one was coming.

"You worry too much," I replied as I tacked a piece of red cardboard to the bulletin board next to the girls' locker room. I stepped back and read the note written on it.

TWO COOL LOOKING 9TH GRADE BOYS WITH TWO EXTRA TICKETS TO THE ROCK CONCERT NEXT SATURDAY LOOKING FOR 8TH OR 9TH GRADE GIRLS TO GO WITH. CALL KIP AT 555-1789.

"I think the 'cool looking' part is a bit much," said Don.

"Hey, it's the truth." I admired my message.

"What if girls call and want to go to the concert with us?" asked Don.

"That's what we want, isn't it?" I replied.

"But we don't have tickets to any rock concert next Saturday."

"A small point, but true," I said. "We'll face that problem if we get any takers."

"No girl in her right mind will probably call anyway," said Don.

I put my arm on Don's shoulder. "Since we all know that the right side of the brain controls the left side of the body"—I paused to look Don straight in the eye—"taking your last statement at face value we can conclude that only left-minded, right-handed girls will call. I can live with that."

"What are you going to do if girls call and want to go to the concert—there's a girl coming!" Don pushed me down the hall. "Let's get out of here."

When we got to the break in the hall I made a sharp turn and looked back to see if the girl was reading the note. To my delight she was.

"She's writing the number down," yelled Don. "Holy cannoli!" I whipped my hand over his mouth.

"Why don't you announce it over the PA," I whispered. "I'm already late for football practice as it is. I'll call you later tonight and let you know if anyone calls."

I couldn't wait to get home from practice. "Any calls?" I yelled as I opened the door.

"Three," said my mother from the kitchen.

I tossed my books on the table and opened the refrigerator to look. "Who?"

"Get those filthy books off my table," she snapped. "Don called. A young girl named Miss Fox, and Mrs. Hoyes, your guidance counselor."

"Mrs. Hoyes?" I scooped up my books and dumped them on one of the kitchen chairs. "Did she say what she wanted?"

"It was something about your being caught in the girls' locker room," said Louis.

"Shut up, Louis," I barked. *She probably read the note and she's calling to tell me I'm suspended for a day, a week, maybe the whole year.* "Is she going to call back?"

My mother handed me a piece of paper. "She said you should call her as soon as you come in. Here's her number."

I took the paper and turned to go upstairs. "Why don't you call her down here?" asked my mom.

"Yeah," chimed in Louis. "We want to hear what you did." Louis covered his face and walked dramatically around the kitchen. "Where did I go wrong with my son Kipper? Maybe I shouldn't have taken his bottle away at age seven."

I waved my fist in the air. "I'll take care of you when I come down." I went quickly into my parents' room and closed the door. Instead of calling Mrs. Hoyes I called Don.

"Hello," said Don.

"Don . . ."

"Did any girls call?"

"Don," I said. I could hear my voice trembling. "I am in deep trouble."

"What's the matter?" asked Don. "You sound awful."

"Mrs. Hoyes called and she wants me to call her back immediately."

"Mrs. Hoyes, the guidance counselor?"

"Do you know any other Mrs. Hoyes?" I asked.

"What does she want?" asked Don.

"What do you think she wants?"

"Maybe she wants to walk around the track with you and talk about rock music."

"What am I going to do?"

"Tell her the track's a little too muddy to walk on now but you would love to play your *Best of the Heavy Metal Animals* album for her."

"Don. This is no time to be funny. What am I going to say to her?"

"I told you not to do it but you wouldn't listen."

"I don't need your telling me what I should have done. Tell me what I should do now."

"Throw yourself on the mercy of the court," said Don. "It always works on TV. Tell her you're sorry. Tell her you'll never do it again. Tell her you'll do work around the school for a week. Tell her your older brother threatened your life if you didn't do it and that the calls are really for him. One of those suggestions should work."

I hung up from Don but my hands and voice were still shaking. I slowly dialed Mrs. Hoyes's number. "Hello," said a female voice. I tried to say hello back but my throat was so dry nothing came out. "Hello?"

"M-M-Mrs. Hoyes?"

"Yes?"

She knows. I can tell by the way she answered yes she knows. I'm cooked. I'm sunk. It's all over. Forget it. Finished, ended, done. "Louis made me do it. It was his fault."

"Who is this?" asked Mrs. Hoyes.

"It's me, Kipper, I mean Jay." *Blame Louis not me.*

"Jay?" replied Mrs. Hoyes still sounding puzzled.

"Jay Scott. My mom said you called and wanted me to call you back."

"Oh, Jay Scott. The reason I called is . . ." She had ignored my previous pleas completely. I was doomed. ". . . I was talking to your brother this afternoon and he said that you might be able to help me out with a problem."

"Help? Problem?"

"Louis told me you were a good photographer. This Thursday evening there is a school board meeting at the school and one of the ninth graders usually takes pictures of the meeting. Unfortunately he has to be somewhere else and Louis thought you might be able to take pictures for us instead."

I let out a long slow deep sigh of relief. "Pictures. Sure I can take pictures. What time should I be back at school?"

"Come to my office around seven-thirty," said Mrs. Hoyes. "And thanks for your help."

I'm going to kill Louis. It's just like him to want to see me squirm. I took the other message out of my pocket and dialed Miss Fox. I wondered why she had been so formal and hadn't left her first name. "Hello, zoo, Kevin speaking."

"Is Miss Fox there?" I asked in a loud confident voice. There was a slight pause so I asked again, "Miss Fox please."

I was not prepared for the man's reply. "This is the zoo, buddy. Miss Fox and Mr. Bear aren't accepting any calls today but Miss Panther is available to talk later." And with that he slammed down the phone.

All I could do for the next minute was stare at the phone and shake my head. *Miss Panther is available to talk later.* I tapped my forehead with the heel of my right hand and slammed the phone down on the receiver with my left. *Mr. Jackass is going to deck Mr. Fox NOW.* Louis was standing next to the refrigerator eating an orange when I stomped into the kitchen. "Why didn't you tell me about your conversation with Mrs. Hoyes?"

Louis smiled. "I figured Miss Fox would tell you what she wanted."

I chased Louis around the kitchen table and out into the yard. "You did that too!" I yelled as I cornered him back by the fence. "You're dead now!"

"Dinnertime," shouted Mom.

A tough choice. Lasagna or Louis. "Mom's cooking saved your life today but watch out after dinner."

"I'm shaking," said Louis.

You should be. You should be.

◄ 7 ►

I usually threaten Louis with bodily harm but never carry it out. This time, I promised myself, I'd do something. It wouldn't be as dramatic as murder but it'd be enough to get his attention.

After dinner I excused myself from the table. "I have to go down to the drugstore to get some school supplies," I said. "Be back soon." I had to make up some excuse to get out of the house so I could go down to the gas station, four blocks away, and get a twenty-pound bag of ice. By the time I got home with the ice my hands were frozen. When I was sure the coast was clear, I snuck into the garage and put the bag of ice in the extra freezer. Then I went upstairs and started my schoolwork.

It was hard concentrating on my homework since

most of my attention was focused on hearing when Louis left his room.

Around nine I heard Louis's door open. I leaned back in my chair ever so slightly and watched him go into the bathroom, turn on the water for his bath, and return to his room to get undressed. I had less than a minute so I moved quickly. I ran downstairs, carried the bag of ice up into the bathroom, cut open the top with a scissors, and dumped the contents into the tub. Whew! I had just thrown the empty plastic bag under my bed and was sitting down at my desk when Louis went back into the bathroom. First I heard him shut the door and then the sound of water running stopped.

I counted on Louis getting into the tub the way he always did. I could picture him straddling the tub with a foot on each ledge and walking backward until his back touched the wall. Lowering himself carefully down to sitting position on the ledge at the end of the tub he would tuck his legs up under him and pretend to be the United States Olympic water slide champion. With his eyes closed he'd be leaning back and would slide slowly into the water.

I counted quietly. "Five . . . four . . . three . . . two . . ."

"Yaaaaaaaaahhhhhhh," screamed Louis.

"Mission Control, we have splashdown!" I triumphantly yelled.

I could hear my parents running from opposite sides of the house up to the bathroom.

"Louis, are you all right?" yelled my mother as she flung open the door.

My father was a step or two behind. "Louis, are you hurt?"

By the time I arrived Louis was out of the tub and wrapped in two towels. His teeth were chattering and what showed of his back and legs were blotches of bright red. Louis looked over at me but didn't say a word. It took all my self-control to prevent me from laughing out loud. *Gotcha.*

"Why did you do that to Louis?" asked my father in a gruff tone.

"Me? I was in my room doing my homework," I replied.

"Your mother and I didn't do it. It had to be you," insisted my father.

I know I shouldn't have asked what I asked next but I just couldn't help it. "Dad, what did one herring say to the other?" I didn't wait for him to answer. "Am I my brother's kipper?"

"Kipper, can I see you in your room?" said my father. I have a way of telling how angry my dad is by counting the wrinkles in his forehead. Serious face, no wrinkles means I'm not mad, I'm just putting you on. Serious face, one wrinkle means I'm slightly irritated. Serious face, two wrinkles means I'm angry and you better have an explanation for why you did it. Serious face, three wrinkles means I'm furious and you better keep your mouth shut or else you might not make it to your next birthday. This time Dad had two wrinkles. I searched for something to say.

"Kipper," he said as we sat down on the bed. "What's the matter with you? I can't believe you did something like that. Where did you dream up such a crazy thing?"

"From you, Dad," I replied without hesitation.

"From me? I told you to put ice in your brother's bathtub water?"

"Not exactly," I replied. "Two weeks ago I heard you and Uncle Craig laughing about the time you put ice in his bath. I figured if you did it to Uncle Craig, then I could do it to Louis."

A big smile covered my father's face. "I told your mother I'd handle this, so look like you've really been reamed out when you see her." Halfway to the door my father stopped. "Come to think of it, Craig got bright red blotches all over his body when it happened, just like Louis. It took two hours for them to go away."

"What else did you do to Uncle Craig?" I asked.

Dad smiled. "You've done enough damage for one day. Do your homework." It was still tough concentrating on doing my homework because I expected Louis to bust into my room any second to get his revenge. It never happened.

Instead, as I was in the middle of my last math problem, I heard a knock at the door. "Phone for you," said my mother.

I went into my parents' room and picked up the receiver, fully expecting it to be Don. "Kip?"

I waved my fists in the air. *It's a girl. Yesssss. I knew it. Kipper, you're brilliant.* "Yes."

"Is this ticket thing for real?"

I crossed my fingers, which makes telling a little fib okay. "Of course it's for real."

"My girlfriend and I are sort of interested but we'd like to meet you first."

My confidence was growing by the minute. "Sounds good to me."

"Since we both have lunch at eleven forty-five . . ." That's the ninth grade lunch period, I thought. "Maybe we could meet tomorrow."

Impossible, we eat seventh grade lunch. "That's fine but . . ." I was racking my brain for a reason why I couldn't do it. ". . . but tomorrow I have to . . ." Have to what? *Come on, Kipper, think.* ". . . go to a . . ." *To a party, to the doctor, to a meeting, yeah!* ". . . meeting for the . . ." *photography club . . . no, she'll think I'm a nerd . . . the yearbook, no she might be on it too . . . the football team, yeah.* ". . . football team."

"What about Friday's lunch?" she asked.

"I meet every lunchtime with the football team. We learn plays and talk over defensive strategies. Maybe we could meet this Saturday at the mall."

"Sounds good. Bring the tickets too. I want to see them," said the girl.

"Sure." I could hear Don saying, "But we don't have any tickets." The small point had just gotten very big. "We'll bring the tickets but how will I know who you are?" I asked.

"Meet us just outside the doors on the third level at noon," she said. "By the way, my name is Andi."

"My name's Kip."

"I know, it was on the note. See you Saturday," said Andi.

As soon as Andi hung up I called Don. "I've got great news."

"What?" asked Don.

"We're meeting two ninth grade girls at the mall on Saturday," I replied.

"What are we going to do about the tickets now?"

"We have three days to come up with something. We'll figure it out," I replied.

"And if we don't?" asked Don.

"You worry too much. We will. We're meeting them at noon. I'll talk to my mom about a ride over and you talk to yours about a ride back. See you in school tomorrow."

I floated back into my room. This was one of the best days of my life. First the polar bath for Louis and now the ninth grade girl on Saturday. I finished the last math problem and got into my pajamas. On my way to the bathroom I passed Louis's room and saw that his light was already out. Something fishy was going on. I picked up the soap and turned on the water. Icy water squirted out from the sides of the faucet. It shot up my sleeves. It trickled down my pants and between my toes. "Damn you, Louis!" By the time I was able to get the water turned off my pajamas were completely soaked and my slippers squished in the puddles that covered the floor. Wet clumps of hair hung in my eyes and one ear was completely clogged. "Damn you, Louis!" I reached under the faucet and peeled off three strips of clear, water-resistant tape that had been fastened over the bottom of both spigots. As I got down on my hands and knees to wipe up the floor I sensed someone behind me.

"You forgot to wash behind your ears," said Louis. "Pleasant dreams, Kipper."

"Just you wait, Louis," I yelled. *Death to Louis!*

◀ **8** ▶

My legs hurt so much I could just barely bend over
and tie my football shoes. And the thought of having to
straighten up after I was finished made my back
tighten up and beg for mercy. At this rate I wasn't
sure how much longer I could last. To make matters
worse I still hadn't solved the dilemma about the girls
and the tickets, and the meeting was only one day
away.

So when Louis walked by with his group of Cro-
Magnon buddies and said, "How's field hockey going,
Kipper, old buddy?" I wanted to rip his head off. *Rrrrr-
rrrip, rrrrrrrrrip,* rip it off and stuff it and hang it up in
my room over my bed. Under it on a metal plaque it
would say:

GENUS: BROTHER

SPECIES: OLDER

Instead I gritted my teeth and stared at the ground until I was sure they had gone. I even cried a little. Not because I was sad but because I was angry and frustrated. I wanted so much to be on the starting team yet I knew I would be lucky to be on the sub-sub-sub-subteam. Just once I wanted to do better than Louis. I hobbled out to the field and got in line for exercises.

"Okay, let's streeeeeeeeeetch," barked Coach Gross. "Legs, legs, legs, legs, come on, streeeeeeeetch." Every muscle fiber in my legs screamed for mercy. "Hip, hop, hips. Shake and wiggle." I expected my butt to fall off and roll down the hill any minute. "Touch those toes. Get the backs loooose as a goose." *Touch my toes? My fingers don't go any lower than my knees.* "Come on, Kipper, you can do better than that." The only way I could do better, I thought, was if my arms were longer. "Neck, neck, neck. You guys should be good at necking. Streeeeeetch that neck." *If he keeps this up I'm going to yell whiplash.* "Everyone, twice around the track. Last one in has to do one more lap."

I kept up with the group for the first lap but I fell badly behind during the second and as usual I was the one who got to do the extra lap. By the time I finished the rest of the guys were already on the practice field scrimmaging, so I sat down under a tree to catch my breath.

"Kipper!" The voice was unmistakable.

I used the trunk of the tree to pull myself up. "You calling me, Coach?"

"Are you joining us at practice today?"

"I was on my way over to the practice," I said.

"You've been taking quite a beating lately," he said.

I didn't think anybody had noticed. "No kidding," I replied as I continued walking toward the field since the coach looked like he was finished talking.

"Wait for a second. I want to talk to you about something else."

I stopped walking and turned around. The coach had a very serious expression on his face so I asked, "Did I do something wrong?"

"No, it's just that . . . This is hard to say because I don't want you to take it the wrong way." I could feel my stomach doing flip-flops and I could hear my heart beating in my ears. "I like you a lot and I think you're trying very hard. I'm going to be announcing the starting team on Monday and you're not going to be in that group."

I shrugged my shoulders and replied, "I really didn't expect to be on the starting team."

The coach bit his lower lip and took a deep breath. "I may change my mind later but at the rate you're developing I don't think you'll be playing in any games this year." I hung my head and started to walk away. "I'm telling you this for a reason. Every other seventh grade boy has dropped out but you've hung in there. I don't want you to get discouraged and drop out too so I'd like you to be the team's manager."

"Manager? You want me to take that wimpy job?"

That job's for the dork who can't walk and chew gum at the same time. That job's for the dweeb who gets put in to play right field when there're two out in the ninth and his team is ahead 30 to 0. "No way."

"It's not a wimpy job," said the coach. "A good manager is very important to the smooth running of a team."

"If it's such an important job tell Louis he can't be the starting halfback because you need him to be the manager and see what he says to that!" I started to walk away but this time toward the locker room.

"I'm not telling you that you have to be the manager. I just thought that . . ."

"You know what you can do with your manager's job . . ." I muttered. I continued walking to the locker room.

"Kipper, come back for a second." I pretended not to hear. "Kipper. Wait, listen." When I got back to the locker room I buried my head in my hand and cried. I didn't even care if anyone heard me. I don't know how long I cried but after a while I got undressed and took a long hot shower. The pelting beads of hot water felt good on my sore body. I was just finishing dressing when the guys came in from practice.

Louis made it a point to come over to my locker as soon as he came in. "Are you okay?" I nodded. "Did you get hurt? I saw you during the warm-ups and then I didn't see you after that."

I shut my locker and started to walk away. "I'm fine. Just leave me alone."

"If you . . ."

I snarled and punched every other end locker on my way out. Once outside I stayed around the side of the school so I could be by myself yet see when the bus came. I sat alone on the ride home.

Louis knew better than to talk to me on the walk home from the bus stop.

"How was practice?" asked my father as we walked in the door.

If I didn't answer I knew he'd be all over me with questions so I said, "Great," and kept walking.

"I'm doing something this year I've never done before," I heard Louis say. "I had three fumbles at practice today and two yesterday. I don't know what's the matter with me."

At least you get to play, I thought as I slammed my door. At least you get to play.

That night I had a tough time getting to sleep but when I finally drifted off into dreamland I wished I was awake. The dream started in an empty football stadium. Two tall pine trees, both of which were bent in half, were somehow growing on the 50-yard line and Louis was tied spread-eagle between them. I stood next to the ropes that held the trees and Louis tied to the ground. I had a scissors in each hand and a big smile on my face. I slowly cut each rope undaunted by Louis's pleas for mercy. I watched as each tree straightened, and one half of Louis flew eastward while the other half floated westward. Then something unbelievable happened. A whole Louis appeared from the east and at the same time another whole Louis appeared from the west. The next thing I knew both

Louises were tied down spread-eagle, I was cutting four ropes, four half Louises were flying north, east, south, and west and then four whole Louises appeared. Before long there were 128 Louises and that's when I woke up in a sweat on the floor, tangled up in my sheets and covers. I didn't sleep much more after that.

◀ 9 ▶

When it comes to getting dressed in the morning I usually grab the first thing I see and throw it on. Red plaid shirts and mustard-colored striped pants or purple-and-orange striped shirts and navy plaid pants are normal combinations for me. Who cares if the colors don't match? Today was different though. I had to look sharp. I had to look cool. I had to be color coordinated. Thirty changes later I settled on khaki pants and a gray and maroon football jersey. I couldn't find my father's deodorant so I had to use my mother's. *Spring Flowers. Makes you smell like a country morning. Yeech.* I even combed my hair.

Later that morning Mom dropped Don and me off at the entrance to the first level of the mall. "Why didn't

you ask your mom to drop us off at the third level?"
asked Don.

"Don't you want to see what the girls look like before we go over and meet them?" I asked.

"How are we going to do that?" asked Don.

"Follow me," I said. We walked on the road that
circled the periphery of the mall. "Let's go over things
one more time so there are no slipups. When the girls
ask to see the tickets, you'll point to me and I'll point to
you and we'll both say we thought the other person
had them. Then in the middle of the week I'll call Andi
and tell her the tickets are lost. If things go well today it
won't make any difference and if they don't it won't
make any difference either." When we got to the edge
of the third level parking lot I motioned for Don to
follow me behind a clump of bushes.

"How do you expect to see what the girls look like
from here? I can just about see the doors."

I pointed to the camera hanging around my neck.
"Do you see this lens? It's a four-hundred-millimeter
telephoto lens." I handed Don the camera. "Now look
and tell me what you see."

Don pointed the lens toward the door. "Wow. This is
amazing. It's like you're right there," said Don. "I think
I see the girls."

"Let me look."

"Wait a second," said Don. "One's tall and blond and
the other's average size with brown hair. This is going
to be great."

Don handed me the camera. "Are you blind, Don?
The tall one's got red hair and the short one is blond."

"Give me that. Look, the tall girl is blond, not red-headed, and she has a Notre Dame sweatshirt on."

I grabbed the camera away from Don and looked again. "You're wrong. The short one is blond and she's wearing a green sweatshirt with flowers painted on it. Let me hold the camera and you look through it."

Don looked through the camera and then shifted the lens to the left. "Kipper, I think we got problems."

"What's the matter?" I asked.

"There are two different pairs of girls. Which one are we supposed to meet?"

I grabbed the camera from Don. "Let me have a look." He was right. Two groups, four girls, and no clues. "What do we do now?"

Don shrugged.

"I know. You'll just have to go up to each girl and ask if her name is Andi."

"What do you mean, I have to ask?" said Don. "You have to ask."

"I'll flip you for it," I replied as I reached into my pocket for a coin.

"No way," said Don. "Your idea, you ask."

Talking to a girl you knew was hard enough in itself. Talking to a mystery girl was out of the question. "What should I say?"

"How about, 'Is your name Andi?' "

"You can't just walk up to a strange girl and ask her that," I said.

"If you can't and I won't I guess we're going home," said Don.

"Then we won't get to meet the girls."

"How perceptive, Kipper. Well?"

Talking to a mystery girl just became part of the question. "Okay, I'll do it but you have to come with me," I said. Don and I started walking toward the mall.

"I was reading in the local paper the other day," said Don, "that the security guards in the mall are on the lookout for some guy who's been going up to ninth grade girls and asking them what their names are. The girls are instructed to yell for security if anything like this happens to them. Don't worry though, Kipper, the chances of them yelling loud enough for the guards to hear them out here is pretty slim. Well, here we are, go to it."

With friends like Don who needed enemies? I knew if I thought about what I had to do it would never happen so I walked over to the tall redhead and blurted out, "Hi, my name is—" Before I had a chance to finish my sentence she turned her back on me and continued talking with her girlfriend. *Don't think, just do it.* I circled around the redhead and positioned myself between her and her friend. "Is your name An—" The two girls turned and walked into the mall.

I walked over to Don, who was standing by the rail doubled over with laughter. "I told you it was the other group," he said. "In fact, I'll go over and ask the tall blond girl myself."

I watched Don as he strutted peacocklike over to the tall blonde. It's amazing how much confidence and courage a person has when they know they're absolutely one hundred percent positively right. I couldn't hear what Don was saying but I did see the girl stop her conversation to listen. At first she looked over at me and shook her head no. Don said something else and she shook her head no again. The third time the girl rolled her eyes, pursed her lips, and blurted loudly, "Get a life," and then hurriedly exited with her friend into the mall.

The only thing redder than Don's face was his ears. Talk about color coordinated. They did clash with his orange sweat socks, though. "What happened?"

"I went up to her and said, 'Hi, Andi. My name's Don and that's Kipper over there.' She looked over at you and said, 'My name's not Andi so please leave me alone.' I guess I should have believed her but instead I said, 'You have to be Andi. Kipper, the tickets . . . remember?' 'I'm not Andi,' she insisted. 'But you have to be,' I insisted back. That's when she left."

"What'll we do now?" I asked, noticing that there were no other groups of girls around. In fact, there were no girls around.

"Are you sure we were supposed to meet them at the third level?" asked Don.

"Sure, I'm sure. Let's wait till twelve-thirty and if they don't come we'll have lunch." Fifteen minutes went by and the girls didn't show so Don and I walked over to the food court and got lunch.

"What do you think happened to them?" asked Don.

"Beats me," I said. "Maybe it's just as well they didn't show up. No telling how they would have acted when they found out there weren't any tickets."

"Isn't that your brother and his buddies over

there?" Before I could turn around to look, Louis was on his way over. "Hi, Louis."

"Hi. I didn't know you were going to be here today."

Louis had a big broad smile on his face. Both his hands were hidden behind his back. "Knock knock," he said.

Don't answer, Kipper. It's a trap. It's a trap. "Who's there?" I replied.

"Andi."

"Andi who?"

Louis pulled his left hand out from behind his back and dropped my crumpled-up notice on the table in front of me. "Andi fooled his little brother again. Psych!" I couldn't believe this was happening.

"Knock knock," said Louis again.

I'm not going to fall for this again. Say knock knock all you want. I'm not answering. "Who's there?" slipped out of my mouth.

"Willy."

"Willy who?"

"Willy ever learn?"

◀ **10.** ▶

"Will you stay after class for a minute, Kipper?" said Mr. Gross as the bell sounded ending math. I wasn't surprised Mr. Gross wanted to talk to me. In fact, I had expected it to happen last week. I sat in my seat and stared at the floor. Coach Gross waited until the room was empty before he began. "You haven't been to practice the past couple of days." What did he expect me to say to that? "Look at me." Mr. Gross paused as I slowly lifted my head. "Hey, I didn't mean to get you upset the other day. I just thought you might get bored just sitting on the bench but if that's okay with you, it's okay with me."

I cleared my throat three times but my voice still sounded shaky. "I was thinking about what you said and you were right, Coach. I'm not very good. It's silly for me to waste my time on the bench."

"You were trying so hard to get in shape and learn the plays before I stuck my two cents in. Won't you reconsider?"

"I can practice day and night for ten years and I'll never be as good as Louis."

"Who says you have to be as good as him?"

A second bell rang. "That's the bell for fourth period. Can you give me a pass?"

Mr. Gross hesitated for a minute and I thought he might be waiting for me to answer but instead he walked back to his desk and filled out a pass. "Think about coming back," he said as he handed me the pass. "Don't use the offer for the manager's job as your excuse for giving up."

For the rest of the day I thought about what Coach Gross had said. *Using the manager's job as an excuse for giving up? I don't understand. I wasn't any good. He said it himself. I don't like hearing it but it's true. I looked like a clumsy padded blimp out on the field. Didn't he say I wouldn't ever play? Didn't he say I'd be bored? When you think about it even if he hadn't said anything to me, what good would it have done me to sit on the bench, never play, and get teased by Louis and his buddies? What I did wasn't an excuse, it was the smart thing to do.*

After school I walked around the halls until I was sure everyone was outside at football practice before I returned my uniform and equipment. I had some time to kill before the late bus was scheduled to leave so I decided to go to the library and do my homework. I was taking my time walking down the hall, looking in classrooms, when I saw this great autofocus camera sitting on the teacher's desk in one room. *The new Westchester 1000. Boy, would I like to have one of those. Wow. Automatic and manual. Built-in flash. Self-timer for two pictures. Built-in motor drive. Zoom telephoto lens.* I held the camera up to my eye. "Looking for something?" said a female voice. A girl was sitting across the room, typing.

I jumped and almost dropped the camera. "I was just looking at it." I laid it back down on the table. "I wasn't going to take it."

"Never said you were."

"Is this yours?"

"No, it's the school's, but you can look at it," said the girl as she returned to her typing.

I raised the camera back up to my eye and, pointing the telephoto zoom toward the back of the room, focused it on the girl. She had short crow-black hair and small bowlike lips. Her eyes were glued to the computer screen in front of her and her body swayed in time to the rhythm of her flying fingers. She reminded me of a famous pianist furiously playing a concerto before a packed audience at symphony hall. I placed the camera back on the table and started to leave the room. "This has everything. How come the school bought such an expensive camera?"

"The PTA bought it to be used by the yearbook staff," said the girl, without moving her eyes from the screen. "You interested in photography?"

"Yeah," I replied. "My father bought me my first camera for Christmas when I was six. He showed me how to develop and print my own pictures when I was seven. Been doing it ever since."

"Want to take pictures for the yearbook?"

"Me?"

The girl looked up from her screen. "You're the only one here besides me."

"Sure," I replied. "I mean, okay I guess."

"We had a photographer last year but his family moved to a different school district. I have to check with the faculty adviser, of course."

Things were moving a little too fast for me. "You mean you really want me to take pictures for the yearbook?"

"Let me have a second to finish this paragraph," said the girl as she returned to her symphonic typing. I stood frozen in the doorway wondering how I got myself into this. Not that it was that bad, mind you. *Taking pictures for the yearbook with this great camera would be fun. It's just that I don't usually jump into things this quickly. Besides, I don't even know the girl's name yet.*

The girl turned off the computer and came up to me. "Hi, my name is Laura."

"I'm Kipper," I replied.

Laura looked puzzled. "Kipper?"

When I get nervous either I don't talk at all or I talk too much. "My real name's Jay but everyone calls me Kipper. When I was born my brother wanted a dog. Instead he got me so he named me Kipper for the . . . forget it."

"For the what?" she asked.

". . . for the dog around the corner named Kipper. Pretty dumb, isn't it?"

"Older brothers can be pretty dumb," said Laura. "I should know, I have one."

"How much older?" I asked.

"A year and a half. He's in tenth grade now. About the pictures, I was filling in as photographer until we got someone else. I don't know what kind of pictures you take but they have to be better than mine. Will you do it?"

"I guess so."

"I'll be talking to the adviser on Monday. I'm sure she'll say yes so stop here after school and you can pick up the camera. You'll have all week to learn how to use it. The first game is Friday."

"I know," I muttered.

"What did you say?" asked Laura.

"I said I'll see you Monday." *Me take pictures for the yearbook? Sounded good. Really good.*

◀11▶

"Why did you quit the football team?" asked Louis. *It's just like Louis to ask that in the middle of dinner right after Dad had announced he had a horrible day at work. He'd probably ask a raging bull if he'd like to see the new red sweater I got for my birthday.*

"When did you quit the football team?" asked my father.

"I thought you were enjoying it," chimed in my mother.

All eyes were on me. I had a few ways to go now. I could be honest and tell them what happened with the coach. I could be sort of honest and tell them that I was cut from the team and hope that Louis didn't open his big mouth. Or I could be sort of, sort of honest and tell them I had too much schoolwork to do so I had to drop out. "I was too tired when I got home from practice and I was having a hard time getting my work done."

"You had time enough to put ice cubes in the bathtub," said Louis.

It's wonderful having an older brother who's so helpful. "Shut up, Louis." I punctuated the end of my sentence with a kick to Louis's shin.

"Kipper just kicked me."

He's such a loudmouth baby. "Shut up, Louis. I did not!"

"I have more work in ninth grade than you do in seventh and I manage to get it done."

There was a sarcastic tone to my answer. "Good for you."

"Really, why did you stop?" pressed my father.

"I told you I had too much work to do. I don't want to talk about it anymore. Okay?" An uncomfortable silence fell over the table and the clanking of the knives and forks on the plates sounded irritatingly louder. I looked over at Louis and scrunched up my face at him. He scrunched back.

"Dad and I have a surprise for you boys." At that moment I could have cared less. "Dad has a one-day trade show in New York this Sunday and we're going to ride up there with him. There's an arts and crafts exhibit on Columbus Avenue this weekend that I'd like to go to and there are some neat stores that I think you might enjoy seeing too."

My mom's idea of a neat store is a clothing store or a shoe store. Big deal. Arts and farts too. I hate crafts

shows. Reminds me of projects I did in kindergarten.
"Can't I stay home?"

"Yeah, do we have to go?" *At least Louis and I agree on something.* "We'll be okay home alone."

"Pale green rug," I whispered under my breath. Louis kicked me under the table hard. "Louis kicked me for no reason." I tried to kick him back but he blocked it. I waited a minute and tried again.

"Ow, cut it out, Kipper," he moaned.

"Ow," I yelled and jumped up as if I had been just kicked again. "Louis kicked me." I looked over at my parents for a response.

"Boys, will you cut it out?" said my mom and dad in unison.

"I didn't do anything," protested Louis.

That's Louis. He always says he never does it. Me? Sometimes I just keep quiet, not saying I did and not saying I didn't. That's better than denying it all the time.

But this back and forth stuff is nothing new for Louis and me. Half the time it's out in the open. He swings at me, I swing back at him, he trips me by accident, and I trip and accidentally fall into him.

The other half of the time our battles are less obvious. Not less effective but less obvious. For example, Louis is an expert at giving noogies. He'll sneak up behind me just after I've gotten a haircut, get me in a headlock, and rub his knuckles into my head. Ouch! I counter by sneaking up behind him and flicking my finger into his earlobe. I call that a swat. Louis likes to drill a raised knuckle into my arm and give me a dead arm. You can also do it to the thigh but then it's called a dead leg. He's not safe though because he knows that somewhere, sometime, someplace I'm going to walk by him and grab the skin on the inside of his thigh. I'm the master at horse bites. Since Louis is still stronger than me, I have to watch out every time we shake hands, because you never know when Louis will squeeze my fingers and put on the finger crusher. He has to be on guard for me too because if I catch his hands on the table I smack his knuckles with the curved part of a spoon. I call it a flip. Louis calls it major pain.

I picked up my plate and put it in the sink. "I'm going up to do my homework."

"I made a fresh sour cherry crumb pie. Don't you want a piece?" asked my mother.

"Maybe later," I said.

"You probably won't even come to the games now that you're not on the team."

Louis doesn't give up, does he? "Not only will I be at the games but I'll be standing right down there on the sideline."

Louis started to laugh so hard he couldn't control himself. "You're going to be the manager of the team. I am so embarrassed. I may have to change my last name."

My father patted me on the back. "You never told us you were team manager. Congratulations. Now we know why you haven't been at practice."

"I'm *not* the manager," I insisted. "Only wimps take that job. I'm going to be taking pictures for the year-

book . . ." *What if the adviser doesn't want me because I'm only in seventh grade or she doesn't think I
can do the job or Coach Gross tells her not to use me
because I wouldn't be manager? What am I going to say
then?* ". . . starting with Friday's game." I turned to
look at Louis. "If you're nice to me maybe I'll take
some pictures of you." *Taking pictures was better than
playing. Wasn't it? Or was that an excuse too?*

◂12▸

I got the yearbook photography job. Knew I would. Never a minute's doubt. I don't know who was more nervous about the first game, Louis because he was playing or me because I was taking pictures. We took turns in the bathroom in the morning and I met him again twice in the school bathroom.

"Don't expect to be in any of my pictures today," I told him every time I passed him in the hall. He never cracked a smile. Louis is definitely no fun when he's worried.

I got out early from last period and went to the yearbook room to get film. Laura was there as usual, typing away. "Do you live here?" I asked.

"Feels like it," she replied.

"Do you do anything besides the yearbook?"

Laura looked up from her computer. "I like pro football and I watch the games on Sunday."

"So do I." *Want to come over and watch a game sometime? It'll never happen.*

"I go to the movies a lot and I like music," said Laura.

"So do I." *Maybe a movie? Probably no chance.* I spoke as I went into the closet and got three rolls of film.

"Take a lot of pictures," said Laura. "I'd rather have too many to choose from than not enough." I put two more rolls in my pocket and went out to the field. *Laura is all right but certainly not interested in me.*

Both teams were warming up (click) and the stands were slowly filling with parents and students. I positioned myself on the 35-yard line down from our players' bench so I wouldn't have to deal with Coach Gross. A couple of times before the game started I thought he might be staring at me but I pretended not to notice. My parents arrived just in time to see Louis, who was one of the captains, take part in the coin toss. (Click.) We lost and had to kick off. (Click.)

The first quarter was pretty boring, with neither team doing much. I got some pretty good shots (click-click-click-click) of the cheerleaders and one (click) of the band. Midway through the second quarter, we had the ball on the 25-yard line and Louis took a handoff around the right side (click-click-click-click) and scampered 10 yards to the 15 (click-click-click-click-click-click-click). On the next play Louis took a handoff around the left side (click-click-click-click-click-click) and fumbled (click-click-click-click-click). Fortunately for us, one of our players recovered the ball (click-click-click) and we scored on the next play (click-click-click).

It's a good thing nothing else happened in that half because I had to change film. The second half was much like the first. Although Louis scored the second and winning touchdown he had two more fumbles. "Smile," I yelled as he walked off the field. "This is for the October first *Sports Illustrated* cover." This time Louis didn't even look at me. Louis is definitely no fun after three fumbles.

My parents took us out for dinner to celebrate the victory but Louis was in no mood to cheer. "I played a lousy game," he repeated over and over to everything my parents said to make him feel better.

Louis was still complaining about his performance in the game when we drove up to New York on Sunday. "I already have seven fumbles this year and I'll probably have twenty more before the season's over."

Maybe logic would work. "With four games left you'd have to have five fumbles a game to end up with twenty more. You carry the ball about fifteen times a game, which means that every third time you'd fumble the ball. You'd have to be spastic for that to happen."

"So you think I'm so spastic I'm going to fumble the ball every third time I get it. Thanks for the vote of confidence."

"I didn't say that," I replied, sorry that I had tried to help at all.

"I was here. I heard what you said."

"Kipper didn't say that," chimed in my mom.

"You always take Kipper's side," said Louis.

"You're just upset over the game," said my dad. "Can we try and have a peaceful ride up now?"

"If everyone wouldn't keep bringing up the game I'd be fine," said Louis.

"You're the one that keeps bringing the game up," I replied.

"I'm not talking to anyone anymore and I don't want anyone talking to me."

An uncomfortable silence filled the car, broken only by the occasional noises of irritation and discontent coming from Louis's side of the car. Somewhere between then and the time we finally arrived in New York I fell asleep.

"We're here," said Mom as she shook me lightly. I stretched my arms, arched my back, and let out a low-pitched growling noise that Waldo would have been proud of, before joining Louis outside the car. From the parking lot my father got a bus going downtown to his meeting and we took a bus uptown to the crafts fair.

"You can wander around," said my mother, "but don't go too far. I want to be able to see you at all times. You both brought some of your savings so spend it wisely. See you later."

"Which way do you want to go, Louis?" I asked. He looked away and didn't answer. "Aren't you going to talk at all today?" Still no answer. "Okay, have it your way." I walked over to a table with weird-looking bowls and vases on it. Louis followed. "Looks like something I did in first grade." He wouldn't smile either. On the next table were kaleidoscopes of all shapes, sizes, and designs. I picked up a long skinny red one and looked in. "Wow. Every time you turn this one a different naked girl appears. Wanna see?" Louis kept his hands folded so I put it back on the table and continued down the block. *What a jerk. Although maybe it's better this way. As long as he keeps his mouth shut he can't say something to get me into trouble.*

I thought most of the tables had junk on them. Who knows what Louis thought. It wasn't until we got to the middle of the second block that I saw something that interested me. It was a table with old books, magazines, and comics on it. "I can't believe this," I said as I held up a book. "They have a copy of *Upchuck Summer*. I've been looking for this book for a long time. A lot of the kids have read this at school and they say it's so funny." I paid for the book and was about to go to the next table when a tall man with a shopping bag tapped me on the shoulder.

"Wanna buy an answering machine? Fifteen dollars and it's yours."

I know all that stuff about buying things from people you don't know but fifteen dollars for a telephone answering machine was too good to pass up. "Let me see it."

"There's got to be a catch to this somewhere," said Louis. "You can't buy a real answering machine for fifteen dollars." The man reached into the shopping bag and took out a package heavily wrapped in newspaper and handed it to me. I turned to Louis. "Make him take off the newspaper."

I looked back at the man. "Take off the newspaper."

"Don't you trust me?" asked the man.

Louis had a smug look on his face. "Not really."

"What make is it?" I asked.

"I'll show you," said the man as he ripped off the paper. Inside was a black cardboard box with gold and red trim. Across the top in bold red letters was:

Fujiyama
Answering Machine of the Future

This was the real thing all right. I reached into my pocket for the fifteen dollars.

"Never heard of Fujiyama," said Louis.

"It's a Japanese import," said the man. "You can also use it as a dictating machine or to record stuff from the radio."

"I'll give you ten dollars for it," said Louis.

"Hey, I saw this first. This is my machine."

"I'll go halves with you," said Louis.

"No way. He asked me first."

"You have to share. We're brothers."

This was my chance to be one up on Louis. If he wanted to use the machine he'd have to pay me a monthly charge to collect his messages. "Brothers schmothers," I said as I gave the man fifteen dollars. "This is mine." The man handed me the package and disappeared down the street.

"You're not being fair," said Louis.

"Look who's talking about being fair," I replied. "I ask you to borrow a sweatshirt or a record album and you say 'No way.' Then you come into my room and take whatever you want. Don't talk to me about being fair. In fact, I'm not talking to you for the rest of the day now just like you wouldn't talk to me before.''

"See if I care," said Louis.

Whenever Louis says that he cares a lot. I tucked the answering machine up under my arm and continued walking up the street. For the next hour Louis tried to bug me into talking to him but I didn't give in.

On the bus ride back to the parking lot I told my mother what happened. Boy, was she mad. "I told you never to talk to strangers, let alone buy something from them. Who knows what's in that package." Louis seemed to be enjoying my scolding.

"Aw, Mom, you worry too much sometimes. I'm twelve and a half years old and I'm not going to let myself buy anything stupid. This answering machine will be for the whole family"—and I paused to look over at Louis—"except him. No more people calling up and saying they left a message with Louis and you didn't get it."

"You do that too," snapped Louis.

I ignored Louis's remark completely. "You'll see after it's hooked up. You'll be thanking me instead of yelling at me." I could tell my mom still wasn't happy with what I had done but she didn't say anything more about it.

Dad met us at the parking lot and he wasn't happy about what I did either. He'll change his mind too when it's set up, I thought.

"Aren't you going to open it up and look at it?" asked Louis.

I wanted to open it up and look but just because Louis asked me to I waited for a half hour before I did it.

In the car I turned my back to purposely block Louis's view. I ripped the box open and then peeled off the seemingly endless newspaper coverings. "Let me see. I can't see," complained Louis. The top of the machine had a rough weathered reddish cast to it. "Let me see. I can't see." Louis got up on his knees on the car seat and looked over my shoulder. "Is that the machine?" We both saw what it really was at the same time. "You bought a brick," shouted Louis so loudly that the people in California could hear. "You bought an answering brick."

If I had bought a shovel too I would have gladly dug a small deep hole and crawled in.

"You spent fifteen dollars for a brick?" asked my mother.

I finished pulling off the paper and turned the brick over, hoping to find an answering machine on the other side.

"Maybe you'll learn a lesson from this," said my father.

I searched through the shreds of newspapers around me on the seat and on the floor. Still nothing.

"You're right, Kipper," said Louis. "I think the answering brick should be all yours. I promise never to touch it."

The silence in the car was deafening. I felt stupid, dumb, and idiotic.

Louis looked me straight in the eye. "Ha ha. Wait till I tell my friends about this."

Whenever Louis and his friends found out about someone else's misfortune they all banded together and tried to make things worse for that person. Right now I was that person.

◀ 13 ▶

Since the ride home Louis and his obnoxious friends hadn't said one word to me about the brick and it was already Wednesday.

"Want to go to the mall after school?" asked Don at lunch.

"Sorry, but I can't. I have to stay after school today and develop the pictures from last Friday's game."

"Thought we might do a little girl hunting. That's okay. If I find anyone I'll ask her if she has a friend," said Don.

"I've given up looking for girls. No one's interested in me. The girls these days are going for ordinary looking guys so us handsome ones have to suffer."

"Gotta go," said Don. "I'll call you tonight."

After school I went down to the yearbook room.

Laura was there of course. "You said there was a place to develop these pictures."

"It's down the hall," she replied. "I'll walk you down."

Halfway down that hall Laura pointed to a door. "This used to be a supply closet but the school converted it into a darkroom. It's usually pretty cold in here since there's no heating duct," said Laura as she unlocked the door. I turned to shut it but she followed me in. They had everything in there. Developing trays, chemicals, paper, one of the newest model enlargers . . . everything.

I took the undeveloped film out of my pocket and threw it on the counter in front of me. I found developing reels on a shelf off to the side and was about to turn off the lights and load the film on them when I realized Laura was still in the room. "I have to shut the door and turn out the lights now."

"I'll do it," she replied.

It's not cold in here at all. It's roasting. "You're staying in here?" I asked.

"I always wanted to learn how to develop film. You don't mind, do you?"

Where did I put those developing reels? They're not on the counter, they're not on the shelf, they're . . . they're in my hands. "N-n-n-no," I replied as I pulled the door shut and turned off the lights. Loading the film on the developing reel had to be done completely in the dark. "Not much to see, is there?" I joked. "After I wind the film on the reel and start the developing process I'll show you how to do this with a piece of film that's already exposed." The silence was intermittently broken by my quick, shallow breathing and Laura's slow, regular breathing.

Once all the film was loaded and developing I got a long scrap of film from the floor and showed Laura how to mount it on the reel. Initially she had difficulty starting so I got behind her, put my arms around her, and manipulated her hands. I was sweating like I had just run a mile. *What's the matter with me? Maybe I'm coming down with something.* Laura still hadn't caught on when the alarm signaling the end of the development process went off. "I'll have to show you how to do this some other time."

From then on Laura seemed content to watch me. My sweating had subsided a little but I knew I still wasn't feeling right. It wasn't until I was out of the darkroom and sitting on the bus platform outside that I started to feel like myself again. An hour and a half virus? Was there such a thing?

When Louis and I got home my mother told me there was a package for me on the kitchen table. It was a small rectangular box, wrapped. In the return address space were the initials "TT" and under this were the initials "RF." The box was very light and I shook it. Inside it sounded as if something was rolling around.

"What is it?" asked Louis.

"I have no idea," I said as I pulled off the paper and opened the box. Inside was a large stone and the following note:

Tele Tronics
Leading the Way in Telecommunications

Dear Sir,

When you bought our super deluxe answering machine last week we forgot to include our long range remote control device. This device is capable of retrieving the messages from your answering machine through any ordinary telephone.

We regret any inconvenience we may have caused you. Hope you are enjoying your machine.

Sincerely,

Rocco Fettucini
President, Tele Tronics Corp., Inc.

Louis fell on the floor, rolled around, and laughed uncontrollably for fifteen minutes.

I was not amused.

The next day after school there was a letter for me on the kitchen table. In the return address space were the initials "TT" and under it the initials "RF." The letter read as follows:

Tele Tronics
Leading the Way in Telecommunications

Dear Sir,

As a special bonus for purchasing our super deluxe answering machine we are sending you a

high-tech telephone system. It is being shipped to you under separate cover. We hope you enjoy this bonus just as much as we enjoyed sending it to you.
            Sincerely,

            Rocco Fettucini
            President, Tele Tronics Corp., Inc.

Two days later a package the size of a shoe box appeared on the kitchen table. Louis and his smirk were there to see me open it. Inside were two soup cans whose bottoms were joined by a long piece of black twine.

This time Louis and my mother laughed for fifteen minutes. Even Waldo looked like he was smiling.

The straw that broke the camel's back came that night. I was finishing up my homework when Don called. "Why didn't you call me back?" he asked.

I was fuming. Louis had forgotten to give me a message again. "The jerk never told me you called."

"I didn't talk to Louis," replied Don. "I left a message on your answering machine."

I was steamed. "How do you know what happened?"

"Louis told me yesterday in school. He told me that his other friends sent you stuff already and if I wanted to get in on the fun, here's what I could do. I'm sorry, it was too good to pass up."

"Boy, would I like to do something to get back at Louis and his friends," I said.

"Do you have brownie mix at home?" asked Don.

I looked in the pantry and found two boxes. "Two boxes." *Good ol' Mom.*

"Good," said Don. "Listen carefully, I have a great plan."

◀ 14 ▶

After school on Thursday Don rode home with me on the bus. On our way from the bus stop we visited the drugstore.

"They're in a yellow and brown box and they should be right here," said Don as we walked down aisle two in the drugstore.

All I saw were cold remedies, cough syrups, and nose sprays. "I don't see them," I said. "What are they called?"

Don scratched his head. "I think it's Regubuds, or is it Irregubuds? I'm not sure."

"I don't see anything by that name at all. Maybe they're out of them."

"Let's check the other aisles," said Don. "Maybe they moved them to another place." Don and I walked up and down every aisle but we were unable to find anything that resembled what we were looking for. "Ask the pharmacist if they have them."

"How can I ask him for something if I don't know what it's called?"

"Easy," said Don. "Describe the box and tell him that you want the chocolate buds that help people go to the bathroom."

"I can't tell him that," I replied. "It's too embarrassing."

"The pharmacist deals with this stuff every day. He won't think twice about it."

I wasn't crazy about asking, but if I wanted to get back at Louis, I had no choice. Don and I walked up to the counter. There was a woman behind the counter writing something on a pad. "Can I help you?" she asked.

I cleared my throat and mumbled, "Can I speak to the pharmacist?"

"I'm the pharmacist," she replied.

I gulped and turned to Don. "What was it we wanted?" Don whispered something about buds in my ear. "Chocolate buds," I replied.

"They're in plastic bags over by the candy counter," said the pharmacist.

Don whispered in my ear again. "That's not exactly what I want," I said. "I want the chocolate-flavored buds you eat when you have trouble, uh, when you're con—when you can't go."

The pharmacist looked puzzled. "When you can't go where?"

"Um . . . to the . . . you know, when you've got to . . ." Bathroom just wouldn't come out. I could use one of those buds right now to cure my constipation of the mouth.

The pharmacist smiled. "I think I know what you want. You want Regubuds."

Don nodded his head and said, "That's it."

"There's a powder too," said the pharmacist. "It comes in Swiss chocolate, vanilla, and strawberry."

"No, I want the . . . uh . . . the buds."

"They're in a brown and yellow box in aisle five," she said. "You can pay for them at the front counter."

There they were in aisle five, just as she said. "They look just like chocolate chips," I said.

"That's the idea," said Don. "Pay for them and let's get home. We have brownies to make."

The house was empty when we got home. I figured we had an hour before everybody returned. The instructions on the brownie mix were simple and the batter was mixed in fifteen minutes. "How many of the Regubuds do you think we should put in?" I asked.

"Half the box," said Don.

I poured in half the box but it didn't look like enough so I put in the rest. I spread the mix into a pan and put it into the oven. "It says they will be ready in a half an hour. I can't wait until tomorrow at about this time. The team will just be coming into the locker room after their game. Louis will see a plate of brownies sitting on the bench in front of his locker. There will be a note taped to the plate that will say 'Congratulations on a great victory.' Louis and all the guys on the team that teased me about the answering machine will dig into the brownies. In fifteen minutes they will experience some of the greatest end runs in history. Revenge will be mine."

Don and I laughed out loud until the brownies were finished baking. I waited till they cooled and then cut them into squares. "Mmmmm. They smell good enough to eat. Louis and his friends should love them." I scooped the squares out of the pan and put them on a paper plate, which I covered and put in the dining room so no one would notice it. "Thanks for your help, Don. I'll call you as soon as Louis gets home and tell you how things came out."

That night at dinner I didn't talk to Louis much. I was afraid I would burst out laughing. After dinner I sprinted up to my room and shut the door. I had a lot of homework that night and I didn't get to go downstairs for a snack until nine. As I neared the kitchen I heard a lot of female voices coming from the den. It was my mother's weekly bridge game.

If there is one thing I hate it's having a group of ladies make a fuss over me and I knew that's what would happen if my mother saw me. I snuck into the kitchen unnoticed and quietly collected a bag of pretzels, an apple, and a can of soda. On my way out the door Waldo saw me and started to bark. I reached into the bag of pretzels and flipped him a pretzel to shut him up. Waldo, with the pretzel in his mouth, disappeared into the den.

I heard my mother ask, "Waldo, where did you get that?" and before I could reach the stairs she was in the hall. "Oh, Kipper. You gave Waldo the pretzel. Why don't you come into the den and say hello to the ladies?"

I scrunched up my nose and pursed my lips. "I still have a lot of homework to do."

"This will only take a minute. Come." I reluctantly followed my mother into the den. "You know Mrs. Rodos, Mrs. Rifkin, Mrs. Marbach, Mrs. Friedenberg, Mrs. Singer, Mrs. Rackow, and Mrs. Sable."

"He's so big."

"He looks just like you."

"How's school?"

"Soon he'll be taller than you."

I didn't try to answer. Instead I nodded and smiled and hoped that this ordeal would end soon.

"Your mom showed us the photographs you took of the sunset. They're gorgeous."

"Thanks," I replied. "I've got to go up and do homework."

"I'd never hear that from my son."

"What a gentleman."

I turned to go. "Kipper, did you make the brownies I found in the dining room?" I froze. "I didn't think you would mind if I shared your cooking talents with the ladies. I'll make you another batch tomorrow."

"He's a baker too?"

"He loves to cook," said my mother. "Don't you?"

"He'll be a great catch for a girl someday."

Mrs. Sable walked over and handed me a brownie. "Want to taste some of your handiwork?"

This had to be a bad dream. Not only wouldn't I

have my revenge on Louis but I would be responsible for sentencing eight ladies to hard time in the bathroom. "No thanks. I have to go."

I had to go—*they'd* have to go!

I felt awful. Should I go back and tell my mother what I had done? Most of the brownies had already been eaten. It was too late. The ladies would have a dynamite time tonight and I was to blame. I knew it wasn't right to seek revenge on Louis but why did I have to be punished in such a crappy way?

◄15►

The next morning my father greeted Louis and me for breakfast. "Your mother was up all night running to the bathroom with an upset stomach. Must have been something she ate."

I slumped down in my chair although I really felt like crawling under the table. I could see the same scene being replayed in seven other houses. Seven fathers telling an undetermined number of hungry young kids that their mothers would not be down for breakfast. All done in by my dynamite brownies.

I told Don the story at lunch. "It could have happened to anybody. Forget about it."

"That's easy for you to say because it wasn't your brownies blasting their way through the intestines of eight unsuspecting mothers."

"It was my idea," said Don, "so I'm partly to blame."

"Actions speak louder than ideas," I said, "and I made them. How can I ever look my mother in the eye again?"

"She probably won't be out of the bathroom before Monday and by that time . . ." I grabbed Don by the collar and twisted his shirt. He pried my hand away and said, "Only kidding, Kipper. Listen, I got a great idea. After the football game let's go over to the mall. Friday is always a good day for fox hunting."

"I'm not in any kind of a mood to go. I'm going outside to walk around by myself." When I went back to my next period class all I could think about was mothers and brownies and I got yelled at by one teacher for not paying attention. In the last period of the day I got a minus for not having my homework. I told the teacher I did it but left it on my desk at home, which was true, but she gave me the minus anyway.

The minute I walked into the yearbook room to get my camera and film Laura asked, "Are you okay?"

"Huh?"

"I'll get someone else to take pictures if you feel sick," said Laura.

"I'm fine," I replied. "Do I look sick?"

"You know when a virus is starting to make you feel sick and you are just beginning to ache, that's how you look."

I forced a smile. "See, I feel great. Gotta go to the game. See ya." I went into the bathroom before going out to the field and looked at myself in the mirror. Yeech. I could see what she meant. My eyes looked red and puffy and my face was covered with red blotches. Maybe I was coming down with something.

I walked out onto the field and sat down on the empty team bench. The fresh air felt good on my face as I loaded the film into my camera. I saw my parents sitting on the 50-yard line and I waved. Seeing that my mother had returned from the porcelain prison made me feel a little better. I walked to the center of the field where the team was warming up. (Click-click-click-click.) The whistle blew to start the game and I took my position on the sideline.

During the first quarter Louis fumbled the ball twice (click-click-click-click) and the coach made him sit on the bench until after halftime. The telephoto lens brought me next to him on the bench. Every time the boy who went in for him got the ball, Louis pounded his fist on the bench and kicked the ground with his foot. I started to walk over to him but changed my mind when he got up and kicked over one of the water buckets.

Louis scored a TD in the third quarter (click-click-click) and was playing pretty well in the fourth until he fumbled on a third down and goal (click-click-click-click) and the other team recovered. (Click-click.) We won anyway but it could have been a slaughter.

After the game I caught up with Louis as he was walking off the field. "Forget about it. You'll do better next time. We won anyway so it didn't even matter." Louis didn't even acknowledge my presence. Instead he quickened his walk and left me standing by the visiting team's bench. I walked over to my parents, who were still sitting in the stands. I could tell they were upset too.

"Looks like his fumbling is getting worse, not better," said my father.

"Don't say that to Louis, dear," chimed in my mother. "He's upset enough as it is."

My father turned and without saying a word gave Mom a "what do you think, I'm stupid?" look. "I think we'd better have dinner at home. I don't think Louis will be in any mood to go out tonight. Kipper, are you coming home with us or going home on the bus?"

Whenever Louis gets like this he's impossible to be with. "The school's going to be open late tonight because of the eighth grade dance. I think I'll stay here and get my picture developing and printing out of the way."

"What about dinner?" asked my mother.

"I'll grab something when I get home. If I call around eight can someone pick me up?"

"I'll pick you up," said my father.

When I got to the yearbook room it was empty. I went into the darkroom, got everything ready, and was just about to turn off the lights and close the door when Laura appeared.

"Feeling better?" asked Laura.

"I guess so," I replied.

"Mind if I come in while you develop the film and print the pictures?"

"I don't mind. Come on in."

Laura pulled in a chair and sat down. "What was the matter with you before?"

I began wrapping the film around the developing ring. "Nothing really."

"You don't have to answer this but does it have to do with something in school?"

"No."

"Something at home?"

"No."

"I get this way when my parents give me a hard time at home," said Laura.

"It's not that. It's just . . ."

"Just what?" said Laura. "Come on, you started."

"It's just that nothing's going right for me this year," I replied.

I saw the outline of Laura moving her chair closer to the counter where I was working. "What's not going right?" she asked.

The room seemed hotter so I flipped a switch above my head and turned on the fan. "I went out for the football team just like Louis, but I was so bad that the coach asked me to become team manager. I try to do as good as Louis in school but no matter how hard I study he always does better.

"Last weekend I went to New York with my family and I bought an answering machine from a guy for fifteen dollars. I was going to let my parents use it but not Louis. That way I could get back at him for all the things he did to me."

"Have you let him use it yet?" asked Laura.

"When I unwrapped the answering machine it turned out to be a brick."

"You bought a brick?" Laura's laugh was muffled at

first but it progressively got louder and louder. "Sorry for laughing, but what do you mean you bought a brick?"

"It's okay to laugh. Instead of an answering machine the guy sold me a . . . it's too long to go into now. I'll tell you about it in detail some other time. But that wasn't the worst of it. Louis and his friends teased me about it day and night. Don, my best friend, and I thought up this great plan to get back at him and his friends. We made some brownies and put some of those chocolate buds in them that make you go to the bathroom when you're constipated."

"Did they work?" asked Laura.

"Well . . ." Suddenly it all seemed pretty funny and I started to laugh too. "My mom found them in the dining room where I hid them and her bridge group ate them. My mom was up all night and I guess so were seven other ladies . . ." The alarm rang signaling the film was developed so I turned on the lights and poured out the chemicals.

Laura was wiping the tears from her eyes. "That was one of the funniest stories I ever heard."

"It's not so funny when nothing ever works out for you."

"Lighten up. Things can't be that bad. I have fights with my older brother too but they pass. I don't spend my whole life trying to be like my brother or thinking about ways to get back at him," said Laura.

I slammed my fist down on the counter so hard all the bottles rattled. "You don't know what you're talking about. It's different between sisters and brothers and brothers and brothers." I began to pace around in a circle. My hands were waving and pointing. "I don't spend all my time trying to get back at him. I do a lot of other things. And why shouldn't I want to be like him? Everyone says he's the best player on the football team and all his teachers say he's one of the smartest kids in the school." I turned the lights off and began to print some pictures. I was glad the lights were off now because I didn't want her to see how mad I was.

Laura got up from her chair and stood next to me. "Maybe all that's true about Louis. Maybe he is a good athlete and smart in school, but why do you have to be like him? What's the matter with you?"

I didn't know what to say. I was quiet for a long time while I took the developed rolls of film out of the container. I cut the film into strips and hung them up to dry from a wire that spanned the width of the room. *Boy, am I a jerk. Why did I get so mad? She was only trying to help. Way to go. You messed it up again.* I turned on the lights again. Laura was still standing by the counter. My mouth felt dry and the palms of my hands felt wet. "I got to go now. My parents are expecting me home for dinner." *Say something. Tell me I'm a loser, I deserve it.* "I'll be back Monday to print up the pictures."

"Have a good weekend, Jay," said Laura.

She doesn't look angry. She doesn't sound angry. "You too," I replied as I hurried out of the darkroom down the hall to the pay phone. "Dad, can you pick me up?" I wasn't sure about anything.

"Be right over," he replied.

"How's Louis doing?" I asked.

"He's been in his room since he came home. I'll go up and talk to him later. See you soon."

I waited outside on the front steps of the school. I kept repeating, "What's the matter with you? What's the matter with you?" over and over. When my father arrived I still hadn't answered the question.

◄16►

When I got home Louis was still in a foul mood and he stayed that way the entire next day. To stay out of his way, I spent a lot of time in my room, sometimes by myself thinking, and sometimes talking to Waldo. I know talking to a dog sounds crazy, but somehow when I'm done it makes me feel better. Whenever I start talking to Waldo, he looks me straight in the eye, cocks his head to the side, and perks up his ears. Waldo is probably the best listener of anybody I know. Besides that he never interrupts, never talks back, and always takes what I say seriously.

Saturday night my parents went out, leaving Louis and me alone together. There wasn't anything good on TV so I grabbed an apple and went back to my room. Waldo followed and he jumped up on the bed beside me when I lay down. "Nothing seems to be going right these days, Waldo," I said. "I want to get a girlfriend, like Louis, but I've struck out with that so far. I'm trying my hardest in school and all I can ever get are C's and a couple of B's." Waldo opened his mouth wide to yawn and a high-pitched squeak came out. "You're right, I could try a little harder. I could study a little more." Waldo squeaked again. "Back off, I hear you. Let me ask you something. Do you think it was fair for Louis and his friends to bust on me like they did for buying that brick?" Waldo rested his chin on his paws and raised his eyebrows. "So you agree it wasn't fair." I patted Waldo on the head. "I knew you'd be on my side." I rested my head on the bed next to Waldo's. "Who's your best friend?" Waldo inched closer until our faces were touching and then he began to furiously lick my nose. I tried to bury my face in my hands but he burrowed his way in and continued licking my nose, ear, and cheek.

After a few minutes Waldo stopped licking me and he jumped off the bed. He walked over to the door and began to scratch it. "Oh, you have to go outside," I said. I opened the door and followed him downstairs. I unlocked the back door and let Waldo out. As I was closing the door I felt some planelike object strafe my hair and zoom into the house. I slammed the back door and walked into the kitchen. At first I didn't see anything. I was about to go into the dining room to look when the plane strafed my head again. *"Louis!!!!"* I yelled at the top of my lungs. *"Louis!!!! Come quick!!!!"*

I heard Louis's door fly open and hit the wall, then

thundering footsteps as he galloped down the stairs. "Kipper," yelled Louis, half out of breath as he bounded into the kitchen, "are you all right?"

"I think a bird flew into the house when I opened the door to let Waldo out," I said.

"You must think I'm pretty dumb, if you think I'd fall for that," said Louis.

"Honest, Louis," I said, "I'm not kidding."

"Then show me the bird," replied Louis.

"Follow me. I think it flew into the dining room."

"You go first," said Louis. We walked into the dining room but there was no bird to be seen anywhere. "See!"

"Maybe it flew into the living room," I said.

"I know you're up to one of your tricks and I'm not in any mood for them," said Louis as he walked back to the kitchen to get a snack. "If you know what's good for you, you won't bother me anymore tonight." As Louis turned to go, the bird zoomed out of the dining room and whizzed past his ear. Louis jumped. *"What was that?"*

"That's the bird I was talking about," I replied. "I saw it go back into the dining room." Louis and I crept up to the entrance of the dining room and looked in. "Do you see anything?" I whispered.

"No," Louis whispered back. "Wait, what's that black bloblike thing on the end of the table over there?"

"Go over and see what it is," I said.

"You go over," said Louis.

"Are you afraid to check it out?"

"No more afraid than you are," he replied. "Let's both go over." Cautiously we approached the end of the table. The black blob looked like a handball at first.

"Pick it up," I said.

"You pick it up," replied Louis.

"You're such a wimp," I said as I reached out to grab it. "My brave brother Louis is afraid to pick up a handba—" Suddenly a head popped up from the back side of the ball—a small black mouselike head. Then long black wings sprouted from each side and the ball took flight. "It's a *bat!!!*" I yelled, and I covered my head with my hands and hit the floor. Louis hit the floor beside me.

"You okay?" asked Louis.

"I think so," I replied. "What'll we do now?"

With our hands still covering our heads we both sat up and looked around. "Do you see it?" asked Louis.

I turned my head in every possible direction. "Nope." We both stood up. "Now what?"

"We have to get it out of the house," said Louis. "But first we have to get something to cover our heads. I heard if it lands in your hair it'll lay eggs and baby bats will be growing in your head. I'm going upstairs to get my football helmet."

The only thing I could find was the wastebasket so I emptied it and held it over my head with one hand. "What now?" I asked Louis.

"Open the back door. You get the broom and I'll get the dust mop and we'll chase that sucker out of this house."

"What if he tries to bite us?" I asked as I opened the back door and got the broom.

"I know something that will prevent it from doing that." Louis opened the pantry door and knelt down and got something. "I think bats are repelled by garlic. Here"—and he handed me several cloves of garlic— "crush all but one and rub it all over your body."

"They're not repelled by garlic," I said. "They're repelled by onions."

"Garlic," barked Louis.

"Onions," I barked back.

"Garlic!"

"Onions!"

Without warning the dive-bombing bat flew between us and we both hit the floor again. "Let's do both," said Louis.

"Good idea," I replied. Louis rubbed his body completely with garlic while I rubbed mine with onions. Then we switched. I got string from the closet and we made two string necklaces with a piece of garlic and a piece of onion on each and hung them around our necks. The only thing that separated us from the finest Italian garlic bread was a sprinkling of Parmesan cheese and five minutes under the broiler.

Louis approached the dining room from the living room side and I went in from the kitchen. We didn't see anything at first. Suddenly the bat appeared from under the table and swooped by at Louis. He swung his mop but missed it completely and knocked two brass candlesticks off the dining room table instead. The bat took a wide turn and headed back toward me.

I took two steps backward and—smash! The head of the broom went through one of the panes of the dining room window. Vroom! The bat circled around again but this time it went into the kitchen and Louis and I raced after it swinging our weapons and laughing. When the bat reached the other side of the kitchen, instead of making a right and going outside, it made a left and flew into the powder room. Louis quickly slammed the door.

"What'll we do now?" I asked.

"You go in and open the window and he'll eventually fly out."

"You go in," I replied.

"No, you," said Louis.

"I got an idea," I said. I got a piece of paper, a crayon, and some tape from the kitchen. I printed a message on the paper and hung it on the door.

BEWARE OF BAT!! PLEASE USE UPSTAIRS
BATHROOM

"Well, what do you think?" I asked.

"I think Mom will get a heart attack when she sees that," said Louis. "One of us has to go in and open up the window. I'll flip you to see who goes in."

"You always cheat when you flip the coin. I'll flip it this time and you call it." I reached into my pocket and took out a quarter. I flipped the quarter up into the air. "Call it."

"Heads!" shouted Louis. The quarter hit the floor, spun around a little, and landed head up. "Heads it is," said Louis. "You go in."

I slowly opened the door and turned on the light.

The sink? No. The toilet? No. I looked everywhere but I didn't see it. I unlocked the window and pushed it open. As I ran back into the kitchen the bat zipped by me but when he sensed Louis standing by the stove he changed direction and went after him. Louis swung his mop in self-defense. Crash! My wastebasket helmet hit the floor. Waldo, tired of running around outside, scampered through the open door into the kitchen. He spotted the bat and immediately began barking at it. We watched as he chased it around the kitchen two times, then out the door into the night.

I quickly shut and locked the door to prevent it from coming back in. "It's gone," I said turning to Louis. "Quick, shut the bathroom window before it comes back." Louis ran into the bathroom and shut the window. When he came back into the kitchen we looked at each other and fell to the floor laughing.

It was five minutes before we could collect ourselves and clean up the mess in the dining room. I left a note for my parents telling them I would explain the broken window in the morning. We each gave Waldo five dog treats for his bravery.

"I'm going upstairs," I said to Louis.

"Wanna sleep in my room tonight?" he asked.

"Sure. Wanna see the new comic books I got?" I asked.

"Why not? We can listen to my new tape," said Louis.

"Sure. Great." I got my pillow and the comic book and met Louis in his room. "You smell awful."

"You don't smell like a bouquet of roses yourself,"

said Louis. "I'm keeping my necklace on until tomorrow just in case the bat or one of his relatives decides to come back."

"Good idea. I already took two showers this week." We had a great time the rest of the night, attacking each other with our pillows and spreading that garlic smell all over the place. We had just turned the lights off when my parents came home.

"The boys are sleeping together tonight," said my mother as she passed Louis's door. "We'll have to ask them what happened to the dining room window tomorrow."

Sniff, sniff, sniff. "I wonder what they were cooking with onions," asked my father.

Sniff, sniff, sniff. "It was garlic," replied my mother.

Sniff, sniff. "Onions," insisted my father.

Sniff, sniff. "Garlic," said my mother as she shut the door to their room.

I nudged Louis's upper bunk with my foot. "Both," I whispered and we fell asleep laughing.

.17.

After school Monday I went to the yearbook room to print the pictures from last Friday's game. I was relieved that Laura was not there. It's not that I don't like talking to her, because I do. It's just that I wasn't in the mood to talk about serious stuff like we did last Friday. Also, that smell was still clinging to me. I went into the darkroom and printed up Friday's game photos. While they were drying, I sorted the pictures from previous weeks into groups.

Band . . . cheerleaders . . . Louis getting the ball, running left, running left, fumbling . . . cheerleaders . . . Louis running right, running right, running right . . . cheerleaders. . . . Other guys running with the ball . . . Louis running right, running right, running right . . . parents waving . . . team exercising . . .

cheerleaders, cheerleaders, cheerleaders . . . Louis running left, running left, fumbling.

The bell on the timer rang in the darkroom just as I finished. I took the new pictures from the dryer and put them into their proper piles. I was surprised to see how many photos I had taken of Louis. The camera had dated and numbered each picture so it was easy to lay them out in sequence on the table in front of me.

As I walked back and forth eyeing the photos for the best shots, something interesting caught my attention. It seemed that every time Louis ran to the left he fumbled but when he ran to the right he didn't. I put all the pictures of Louis running left on the left half of the table and all those of him running right on the right side. It was true: left, fumble—right, no fumble.

Why? It didn't make sense. Maybe the quarterback was handing the ball off differently on the left side than on the right. I found all the negatives of the quarterback handing off the ball to Louis and enlarged the section of the picture containing the hands. I examined each print under a magnifying glass. "The hands look good here, the ball's right where it should be, the elbows bent perfectly, the wrists fine . . . nothing wrong here, next . . . next . . . what about this one . . . nope. Nothing here."

Next I collected all the negatives that showed Louis running right and blew up the section of the picture that showed him carrying the ball. I did the same with the negatives of Louis running left. I put all the run-right prints in a line and all the run-left prints next to them. "Come on! What's going on here! Why's he dropping the ball? Why's he dropping the ball?" I looked around to make sure no one had come in. "Hands good, arms good. What is it? I'll bet the answer's staring me right in the face."

My eyes were starting to water so I put down the pictures and the magnifying glass and walked out into the hall to get a drink. *The answer has to be there someplace,* I told myself, *but where? I've checked everything. There's nothing more to check.* I kicked the wall in disgust.

I walked back and looked at the blowups again. I inspected each one individually to make sure that when Louis ran to the right, his right hand cradled the ball from below, and his left hand steadied it from above, and when he ran to the left his hands were vice versa. "Darn, everything checks out. I give up." I mushed all the pictures into a pile in the center of the table. I wanted to throw the whole mess up into the air. The thought of it made me smile. Why not? I slid my hands under the pile and counted. "One . . . two . . ." Then I saw it. Actually it wasn't what I saw, it was what I didn't see that caught my eye. There weren't any thumbs or fingers wrapped around the ball. Instead his hand was completely flat. I rummaged through the pile and picked out all the run-left prints. Every one showed the same thing. For some unknown reason Louis wasn't gripping the ball with his left hand.

But why? Louis knows better than that. Why isn't he gripping the ball? I asked myself over and over as I collected the pictures to show Louis. *Did he hurt his hand in practice? Not that I know of. Then why can't he grip the . . . The line drive he caught bare-handed in the championship game last August. Was it his left hand? Hmmmm, I think it was. Remember, he complained that his palm was still sore and it hurt to squeeze stuff with his hand. That's it. He probably didn't tell Mom and Dad or the coach about it for fear they wouldn't let him play. What a dope. If he went to a sports medicine clinic they'd probably tell him what to do to get it better and I'm sure they'd have something to protect it so he could still play.*

I couldn't wait to tell Louis I had solved his problem. I carried the photos with me to show him why he was losing the ball. Practice had just ended when I got to the locker room and Louis was sitting, with his back toward me, on the bench in front of his locker. He had his head buried in his hands.

"Louis," I yelled, "I figured out why you're fumbling the ball so much." I ducked as his football helmet sailed over my head and crashed against the lockers behind me. "What's the matter with you? Are you crazy?"

"What do you know about football? You couldn't even make the team."

I was so angry I wanted to run over and rearrange Louis's face. Instead I pointed my finger at him and yelled, "You're a jerk, Louis. A stupid, dumb jerk. I hope you end up sitting on the bench for the rest of the season!" I stomped out of the locker room, crumpling the pictures in my left hand as I went. Halfway down the hall I passed a large gray trash can and with the skill of an NBA guard tossed them in.

On the bus ride home Louis sat in the back with his friends and I sat in the front by myself. When the bus let us off, Louis walked ahead of me and he went straight to his room as soon as he got into the house.

At dinner, during dessert my father asked, "Louis, how was practice today?" At first Louis didn't answer. "Did you have any good runs?" Louis threw down his fork and bolted away from the table. No one said a word for what seemed like a long time. "I guess he fumbled a lot again at practice. I'll go up to talk to him."

"I want to talk to you about something when you come down," I said.

I heard my father walk upstairs, and then there was a long period of silence. Then loud voices and slamming doors and my father came into the kitchen. His face was beet red and he was breathing heavily. When he saw Mom was not there he tromped into the den.

"I give up. Everything I suggest to him he rejects. Then to top things off, he has the gall to say 'What do you know, you're no football coach.' That's when I lost it. I told him I didn't care if he sat on the bench for the rest of the season. I know I shouldn't have said that but he just got to me. Who does he think he is telling me I'm no football coach?" My father suddenly appeared in the kitchen and gulped down a cup of coffee. He turned to me and asked, "You wanted to tell me something?"

"Um, nothing, Pop." I left the kitchen and went to

my room. I guess I should have told my father about my discovery in the darkroom today but I figured Louis wasn't listening to anybody, not even my dad, so why bother? "What should I do now, Waldo?" Waldo opened one eye for a few seconds, yawned, and then fell back to sleep. "Study my math more? Good idea," I replied. As far as the Louis situation went, it was a lost cause.

◀18▶

I passed Laura in the hall the next day and said, "I picked out some pictures I think would be good for the yearbook. I'll show them to you after school."

"I'm glad you'll be there," she said. "I wanted to ask you something."

"What?" I asked.

"I've got to go to class. I'll tell you later."

I wonder what she wants? She probably wants to ask me to take pictures of something. What's coming up? Basketball. Can't wait for that to start. Anything else? The eighth grade dance is . . . let's see, three weeks from Friday. She'll want me to take pictures of that too since I'm not going. Anything else? Nope.

Laura was already there when I came into the room. "Hi."

"Be with you in a second," she said. "I have to finish typing this."

I went into the darkroom and got out the pictures I wanted to show Laura. I spread them out on the table and waited for Laura to come over.

"I like them," she said, "especially the ones of your brother carrying the ball."

I felt good, but a little embarrassed. "Thanks. Where do you want me to put them?"

"I'll take care of them," said Laura as she scooped them up and put them in a folder marked SPORTS PIC-TURES. "Can I ask you something?"

For some reason Laura looked more serious than usual. Had I done something wrong? "Sure."

"You don't have to answer this if you don't want to."

I was beginning to feel a little nervous. "Okay."

"What happened yesterday between you and your brother?"

Had Don told her? How could he? He didn't even know who she was. "How did you find out about it?" I asked.

"A couple of the football players are in my Spanish class and I heard them talking about it. They said Louis threw his helmet at you. Is that true?" I nodded. "Why did he do that?"

You said I didn't have to answer if I didn't want to; well, I don't want to! "Because he's a jerk! That's why." I began to pace back and forth. My arms were flying everywhere. "Louis was fumbling the football a lot and it's because he hurt his hand playing baseball and I had pictures to show him but he threw his helmet at me, so I walked out."

"What?" said Laura. "Football? Baseball? Pictures? What are you talking about?"

"I guess I'm not making much sense, am I? It's just that Louis makes me so mad sometimes that I could kill him. Not really kill him but kill him, understand?"

Laura smiled. "I have an older brother, remember?" said Laura.

"Then you know what I mean. I've already killed Louis off about a million times and I've brought him back to life a million and one times. This time he deserves it, though. You see, last year Louis was the star halfback of the football team. This year things are different. He's been fumbling the ball a lot and the coach even benched him awhile in the last game. Yesterday when I was looking at the pictures of Louis playing I noticed, quite by accident, that every time Louis ran to the left he fumbled the ball." I walked over to the sports folder and took out one of the photos of Louis running. I pointed to the part of the picture that had Louis's hands in it and said, "I couldn't figure out why that was, so I enlarged this part of each print and I saw that Louis couldn't grip the ball with his left hand. I remembered that he hurt his hand playing baseball this summer and then everything made sense. I went down to the locker room to tell him and what does he do, he throws his helmet at me." I held up my thumb and index finger. "I was this close to rearranging his face."

"So you never told him," said Laura.

"I tried but he wouldn't let me," I replied. "It's his problem to figure out now."

"Are you still going to tell him?" asked Laura.

I was getting a little annoyed. Couldn't she understand? "I told you I tried. He wouldn't let me. That's it! It's over."

Laura walked away without saying anything and started typing articles for the yearbook again. *Jeez! I blew it again.* I've said things I probably shouldn't have to Louis and Don before, but I never felt quite like this inside. It's hard to describe. It was a pinch of feeling stupid mixed with a dash of feeling bad, topped off with a layer of embarrassment and regret.

"I've got to go," I said. I walked toward the door, but halfway there I turned around and walked back to Laura. "I was going to ask my father to tell Louis what I found but Louis won't listen to him either. You tell me how to get Louis to listen and I'll do it."

Laura looked up from her typing. "Tell the coach what you found. Louis will listen to him."

"The coach won't listen to me," I said.

"Why not?" asked Laura.

Because, I thought, I quit the team and no coach is going to listen to a quitter. "What coach is going to listen to a seventh grader telling him what's wrong with one of his players? It'll never happen."

Laura smiled a reassuring smile. "You could try," she said.

I smiled back because at that moment I really believed I could. *She was right. And she wasn't mad at me.* "I'll do it tomorrow after school," I said.

"Why not today?" asked Laura.

"I was so mad yesterday I threw away the enlargements and I need them to show the coach. By the time I get them redone today the coach will be gone."

"If I help you," said Laura, "you should be able to get them done by the time practice is over."

What could I say? We finished the enlargements in less than an hour and I was on my way to speak to the coach.

It's funny how fast things can change. I know because as I was standing outside Coach Gross's office, pictures in hand, all the courage and confidence I had when I left Laura a few minutes ago had somehow disappeared. Evaporated, gone, poof, and in its place was an intense feeling of panic. Why was I here? The coach wouldn't listen to me. He'd probably yell at me for interrupting him. Or he'd laugh . . . "Since when did you become a football expert?" Maybe I'd do this tomorrow. Maybe the next day. Maybe never. I was just about to turn around and go when I thought about Laura. What would I say to her if I chickened out? *Well, Laura, I went to see the coach but he had already gone home for the day.* Or, *I went to see the coach but he was sick.* I was getting sick thinking about this. It all boiled down to who would it be easier to talk to: the coach or Laura? That's like asking, "Which would you rather have kill you, a gorilla or a lion?" Frankly, I'd rather have the gorilla kill the lion. Maybe I could get Laura to talk to the coach for me. So, which would it be? Tell the coach why Louis is fumbling or tell Laura why I'm such a wimp?

I knocked on Coach Gross's door. *Maybe he won't be in.* "Come in." I reluctantly opened the door. The coach was sitting at his desk looking over the playbook. "Jay, hi. I haven't seen you since math. What's up?"

I took a deep breath. "Can I talk to you for a minute? If you're busy I'll understand. I can come back later. Maybe I'll come back tomorrow."

"No, come on in. Have a seat."

I walked around to the front of Coach Gross's desk and spread out all the pictures I had taken of Louis running. "Coach, look at this."

◂19▸

As soon as I got home I hid the pictures of Louis in the back of my sweatshirt drawer.

Even though Louis was in a bad mood at dinner, I didn't pay much attention to it. I was still feeling good about my meeting with the coach and I knew that by tomorrow Louis would be feeling better too.

I was in my room studying after dinner when my mom knocked. "Phone call for you."

"Who is it?" I asked, fully expecting her to say Don.

Mom had an impish grin on her face. "A girl."

"A girl?" Probably somebody in one of my classes who needed a homework assignment. I went into my parents' room and shut the door behind me. "Hello?"

"What happened?" asked the voice on the other end of the line.

"What happened what?" I asked. "Who is this?"

"It's Laura. I couldn't wait until tomorrow. What happened when you went to talk to the coach about Louis?"

"He listened," I replied. "He's going to meet with Louis before practice tomorrow and tell him. Then he's going to call my parents and suggest they take Louis to a sports medicine clinic."

"That's cool," said Laura.

"Yep," I replied. The silence that followed seemed to last for hours. *Am I supposed to say something else? Is she supposed to say something else? Since she called me, am I supposed to say good-bye first?* "Yep," I replied again.

"Can I ask you something?"

This time I'm going to say no. "Sure."

"In two weeks is the eighth grade dance. I wondered if . . ."

"I'll be happy to take pictures there," I replied. *I can blow up the pictures of all the cute girls.*

"I wasn't going to ask you to take pictures of the dance," said Laura.

I felt stupid for interrupting. "You weren't?"

"No, I was going to ask you if you wanted to go to the dance with me."

The request took me completely by surprise. "Me? You want me to go to the dance with me? I mean you?"

"Sure. Can you go?"

I have to ask my mother if I can go. That'll impress her. He still has to ask his mommy if he can do things. What am I going to say, then? If I knew that, I wouldn't be asking. Don't panic. Be cool. Now, do I want to go to the dance with Laura? I guess I do. I think I do. I wanted a girlfriend, didn't I? I guess I did. Well, now I have one, I think. I should say yes. No, maybe I should think about it.

"Well," said Laura, "can you go or not?"

If I fumble this opportunity I'll be just as bad as Louis, maybe worse. "I can go," I replied.

"Great, cool, terrific," said Laura. "See you tomorrow."

I hung up the phone and floated into my room. "A girl wants to go to a dance with me," I said to Waldo, who was chewing on one of my old sneakers. "An eighth grade girl wants to go to a dance with me. It'll take me a little while to adjust to dating an older woman. I can handle it, though. Don't you think?" Waldo let the sneaker drop out of his mouth and yawned. "I guess you don't know much about dating. That's okay, neither do I, but I plan to learn."

◄ **20** ►

At the advice of the coach my parents took Louis to the sports medicine clinic, where he received therapy for his hand. The doctor gave him a padded protective glove to use during the games while his hand was healing. In the remaining three games he didn't fumble once and he received the Coach's Award at the football banquet for best all-around player.

In the past that kind of thing would have made me feel jealous of Louis but not anymore. Now I figure if a girl could like me the way I am then maybe I could like myself too. That doesn't mean that things are always calm between Louis and me, because they aren't. It can't be with a brother like Louis. He's always up to something.

For example, the day of the eighth grade dance happened to be my birthday. From the time I got up in the morning I knew Louis was up to something. "If you would like to use the bathroom first that would be okay with me," he said when we met first thing in the hall.

Is he sick? Does he want to borrow something? Has he forgotten he's the older brother? "I'll go first," I replied as I waited a second for something to happen. Nothing did.

At breakfast there was only one cream donut left. Usually Louis steals it before I come down but today he asked, "Would you like the cream donut?"

I reached over and felt his forehead. He didn't feel like he had any fever. "Sure." Again I waited for something to happen but it never did.

After school Louis asked me if I wanted to play basketball, and before we started, he gave me half of his soft pretzel. I pinched myself to see if I was dreaming. After dinner we went upstairs to get ready for the dance. "Would you like to get into the shower first?" he asked.

One of these times I knew Louis would get the best of me but I figured if he's trying to be nice why not go with it. "Sure, I'll go first." While I was in the shower I listened for the door to open and a water balloon to sail over the top of the curtain. As I dried myself off I thought about my date with Laura. Would I dance well enough for her? Would I run out of things to talk about? Would I sweat too much? Would I run out of things to talk about? "It's all yours," I yelled to Louis as I walked down the hall to my bedroom. I stopped because the door was closed and I had left it open. I turned the knob and opened the door slowly with my foot. I waited for something to drop where my head was supposed to be. It never happened. I walked inside and on my bed was a big package with a card taped to the top. I picked it up and shook it. It was fairly light and nothing jiggled. On the front of the envelope was printed:

TO MY BEST LITTLE BROTHER JAY

Inside was a funny birthday card—and all the blown-up pictures I had taken of his hands. On the back Louis wrote:

Jay—Borrowed your red sweatshirt and found these. I should have known the coach wasn't that smart. Thanks. Thought you could use a new one of these. Mom and Dad helped me a little (really a lot) to pay for this.

Love,
Louis

P.S. Notice I called you Jay!

I ripped off the wrapping paper and inside was a new camera and flash, just like the one I used in school. I couldn't believe it. What a great gift. I took the camera out of the box, put film in it, and attached the flash. With only a towel wrapped around me I crept down the hall and sneaked into the bathroom. Louis was humming off-key. I readied the camera and waited for Louis to finish. The water stopped and

Louis pulled back the curtain. He was completely naked and his wet straggly hair hung down in his eyes.

"Louis," I yelled at the top of my lungs. He tried to yank the curtain back but the flash was too quick for him. "Call me Kipper!"